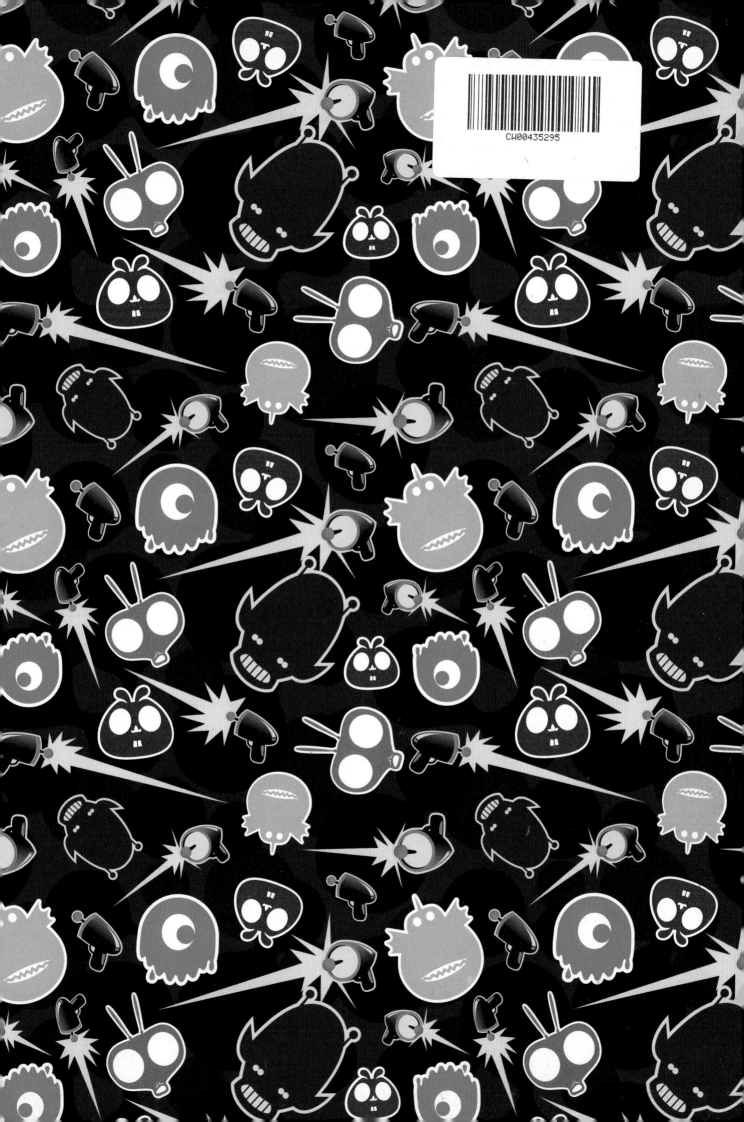

DREAMWORKS
MONSTERS VS ALIENS™

CONTENTS

Published 2009 · Published by Pedigree Books LTD,
Beech Hill House · Walnut Gardens · Exeter, Devon EX4 4DH · books@pedigreegroup.co.uk · www.pedigreebooks.com

B.O.B.

ORIGIN: **Genetically altered tomato**

ACCIDENT: **Combined with chemically altered ranch-flavoured dessert topping at a snack food plant**

RESULT: **Indestructible gelatinous mass**

LIKES TO EAT:
Anything and everything

SPEECH: **Over-enthusiastic**

IDENTIFYING FEATURES: **Blue goo with a single gobstopper eye**

HOBBIES: **Eating**

MONSTERS

THE MISSING LINK

ORIGIN: **Half fish, half ape**

ACCIDENT: **Deep freeze**

RESULT: **Waking after 20,000 years**

LIKES TO EAT: **Small fish**

SPEECH: **Full of bravado**

IDENTIFYING FEATURES: **Scaley body, lots of teeth and lots of attitude**

HOBBIES: **Weight training and kung fu**

DR. COCKROACH PH.D.

ORIGIN: Most brilliant man in the world

ACCIDENT: Invented machine that gave humans the cockroach's ability to survive

RESULT: Became world's first human cockroach

LIKES TO EAT: Household rubbish

SPEECH: Lots of facts and trivia

IDENTIFYING FEATURES:
White coat, bug eyes and antennae

HOBBIES:
Experimenting (also has a Ph.D in dance)

INSECTOSAURUS

ORIGIN: A small grub

ACCIDENT: Nuclear radiation

RESULT: A 350 ft tall Monster

LIKES TO EAT: Japan

SPEECH: Screeches

IDENTIFYING FEATURES:
Very big and very hairy
(and very scary)

HOBBIES: Window licking

MEET THE

GINORMICA

ORIGIN: Susan Murphy

ACCIDENT: Hit by meteorite

RESULT: 50 ft tall giant woman

LIKES TO EAT: Very little – she's watching her figure

SPEECH: Favourite subject is fiancé Derek Dietl

IDENTIFYING FEATURES: Platinum hair

HOBBIES: Saving the world

MONSTERS

WARNING!

ALIEN ALERT

GALLAXHAR

Having destroyed his own planet, the evil tyrant from Outer Space wants to take over the Earth, using his army of clones created from Quantonium – the most powerful substance in the universe. But first he needs to get the Quantonium.

Susan's huge body is full of Quantonium, so when Gallaxhar's alien probe fails to capture her, the four-eyed overlord drags her up to his alien ship to extract it from her.

But he underestimated Susan's amazing strength and her giant cunning, which helps her destroy him and save the planet.

SUDDEN IMPACT

The first sign of trouble came when a planet exploded, causing a shower of meteorites to shoot towards Earth gathering speed as they went. American technicians stationed in Antarctica picked up the presence of one particularly large rock as the monitor bleeped loudly.

"Hey Jerry? You might wanna check this one out. Looks like some type of UFO, and it's heading this way," said one of the technicians.

Wearily his colleague made his way over to the monitor. "How many times do I have to tell you this, UFOs don't exist. And we're never going to see..."

He broke off, not believing his eyes, just as another monitor began to bleep rapidly. "Wow! Its energy signature is massive!" said the stunned first technician.

"What do we do? No one ever told us what to do! The only reason I took this job is because you never have to do anything!" His colleague was already typing furiously on his keyboard, calculating its impact point.

"Looks like... Modesto, California," said the second technician.

The first technician picked up a telephone. "Supernova, this is Red Dwarf! We actually have one! Code Nemoy! I repeat, Code Nemoy!"

It was still dark in Modesto, CA, where Susan
Murphy slept peacefully. While she dreamed,
a strange trio entered the house, walked down
the corridor and found her asleep in bed.
As they leant over Susan she awoke and screamed
in surprise at the sight of her bridesmaids.
They surrounded Susan, snapping pictures of her.
"What are you guys doing here?
It's five o'clock in the morning!" Susan exclaimed.
"Hurry, turn on the TV! Turn it on now!" one said.

As the screen on her TV came to life, an attractive weatherman appeared, standing in front of a map of central California. "...and some early morning fog giving way to sunny skies, seventy-five degrees, a perfect day to stop by the ol' folk art and craft show down at the fairgrounds," said Derek Dietl. "Or a perfect day to marry Susan Murphy." Susan smiled as Derek made the shape of a heart with his hands. "I love you, baby..." he said to the camera. "I love you, too," chimed Susan at the television. "Awww," chorused the bridesmaids.

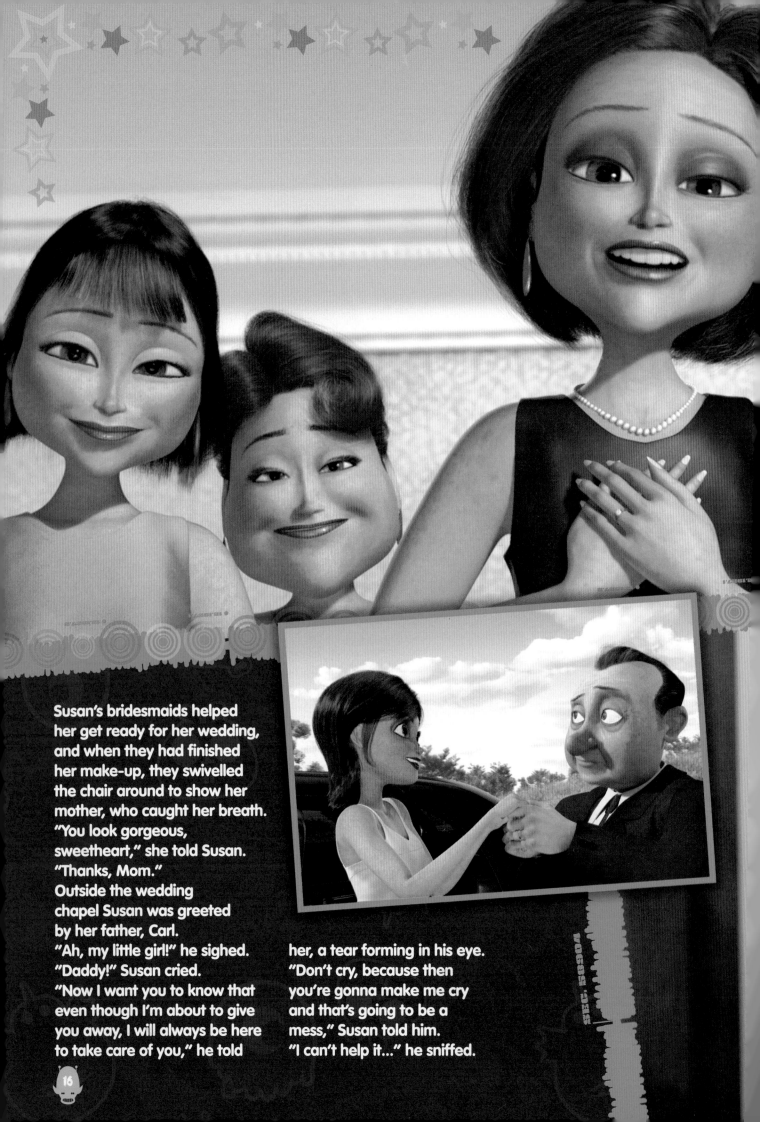

Susan's bridesmaids helped her get ready for her wedding, and when they had finished her make-up, they swivelled the chair around to show her mother, who caught her breath.
"You look gorgeous, sweetheart," she told Susan.
"Thanks, Mom."
Outside the wedding chapel Susan was greeted by her father, Carl.
"Ah, my little girl!" he sighed.
"Daddy!" Susan cried.
"Now I want you to know that even though I'm about to give you away, I will always be here to take care of you," he told

her, a tear forming in his eye.
"Don't cry, because then you're gonna make me cry and that's going to be a mess," Susan told him.
"I can't help it..." he sniffed.

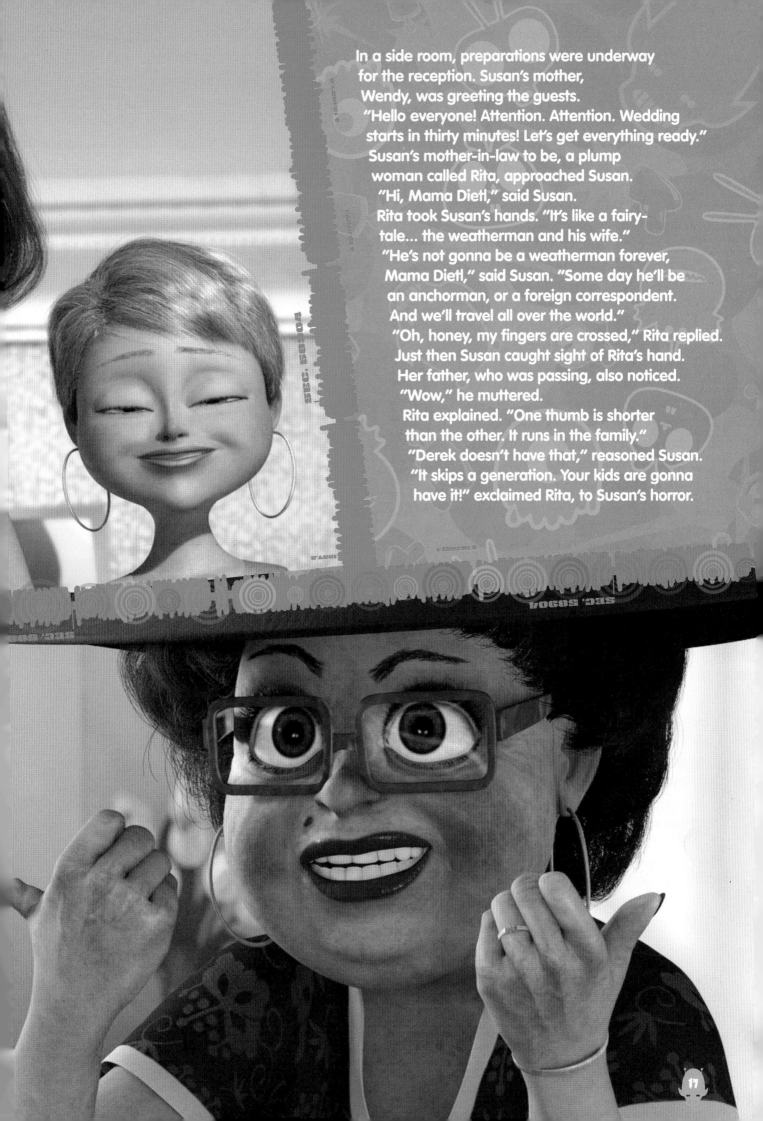

In a side room, preparations were underway for the reception. Susan's mother, Wendy, was greeting the guests.

"Hello everyone! Attention. Attention. Wedding starts in thirty minutes! Let's get everything ready."

Susan's mother-in-law to be, a plump woman called Rita, approached Susan.

"Hi, Mama Dietl," said Susan.

Rita took Susan's hands. "It's like a fairy-tale... the weatherman and his wife."

"He's not gonna be a weatherman forever, Mama Dietl," said Susan. "Some day he'll be an anchorman, or a foreign correspondent. And we'll travel all over the world."

"Oh, honey, my fingers are crossed," Rita replied.

Just then Susan caught sight of Rita's hand. Her father, who was passing, also noticed.

"Wow," he muttered.

Rita explained. "One thumb is shorter than the other. It runs in the family."

"Derek doesn't have that," reasoned Susan.

"It skips a generation. Your kids are gonna have it!" exclaimed Rita, to Susan's horror.

Susan was standing in a gazebo outside the church, enjoying the peace and quiet, when Derek appeared behind her, dressed in his tuxedo. "Wow, you look beautiful," he told her.

Susan spun around to look at Derek.

"So do you. I mean, handsome. I mean... sorry, I'm just a little frazzled. I just spent way too much time with our parents."

"Don't worry, okay? We'll be alone soon, just us," Derek reassured her, taking her hands in his.

"Mmm, eating cheese and baguettes by the Seine, feeding each other chocolate crepes..." dreamed Susan. Derek looked uncomfortable. "Um..."

"Is something wrong?" Susan asked.

"No, no. It's just that... well, there's been a slight change of plans... we're not going to Paris," Derek told her.

"What?! Why not?" she asked.

"Because we're going somewhere better!" said Derek.

"Better than Paris?" replied Susan.

"Oh yeah," said Derek

"Where? Tahiti?" asked Susan hopefully.

"Nope. Fresno!!!" Derek revealed.

"Fresno! Fresno. In what universe is Fresno better than Paris, Derek?" exclaimed Susan. "In the 'I've got an audition to become Channel 23's new Evening Anchor' universe. I got the call from the general manager and he wants me to come in immediately! Isn't that great?" Susan took a moment to hide her disappointment.

"Derek, that's... amazing! It's amazing. Fresno is like a top 50 market, isn't it?"

"Actually, it's 55th, but we're on our way, babe!" He kissed her hand. "Now look, about Paris..."

"Oh, it's okay. It's fine. As long as we're together, Fresno is the most romantic city in the whole world. I'm so proud of you."

"Of us. Not just of me... I mean of course, but we're a team now. You're so proud of us."

"Now get out of here. It's bad luck to see me in my dress."

"Oh come on, you know I don't believe in that stuff," he told her as he headed for the church. "I'll be waiting for you at the altar, the handsome news anchor in the tux. All right? Love ya! There, I said it!"

"I love you, too!" said Susan, and to herself added: "Je t'aime."

Susan was still adjusting to Derek's news when she saw a flash of light appear in the sky. It suddenly zoomed towards her. Susan picked up her wedding dress and began running across the lawn, but her high heels slowed her down and the giant meteorite slammed into the ground close by, covering everything near it in a green glow, including Susan.

Wendy found her looking dishevelled and dazed. "Susan, where have you been?" she asked, pulling her daughter towards the church. "I think I just got hit by a meteorite." "Oh Susan, every bride feels that way on her wedding day," said Wendy. "My goodness, look at you, you're filthy!"

Susan walked down the aisle with her father but when Derek lifted her veil he gasped. "Wow, you're glowing..." said Derek.
"Thank you," said Susan, thinking it was a compliment.
"No. No... Susan, you're like really glowing. You're green."
It was then that she started to grow. She became taller and taller until her back was pressed against the ceiling of the church. "You're all shrinking!" cried Susan.
"Huh-oh, you're growing!" said Derek. "Well make it stop!"
But she was still getting bigger. Pandemonium broke out in the church. The Minister dived through the stained-glass window, the wedding guests fled for the exits and Susan's garter flew off and took out a member of the congregation.

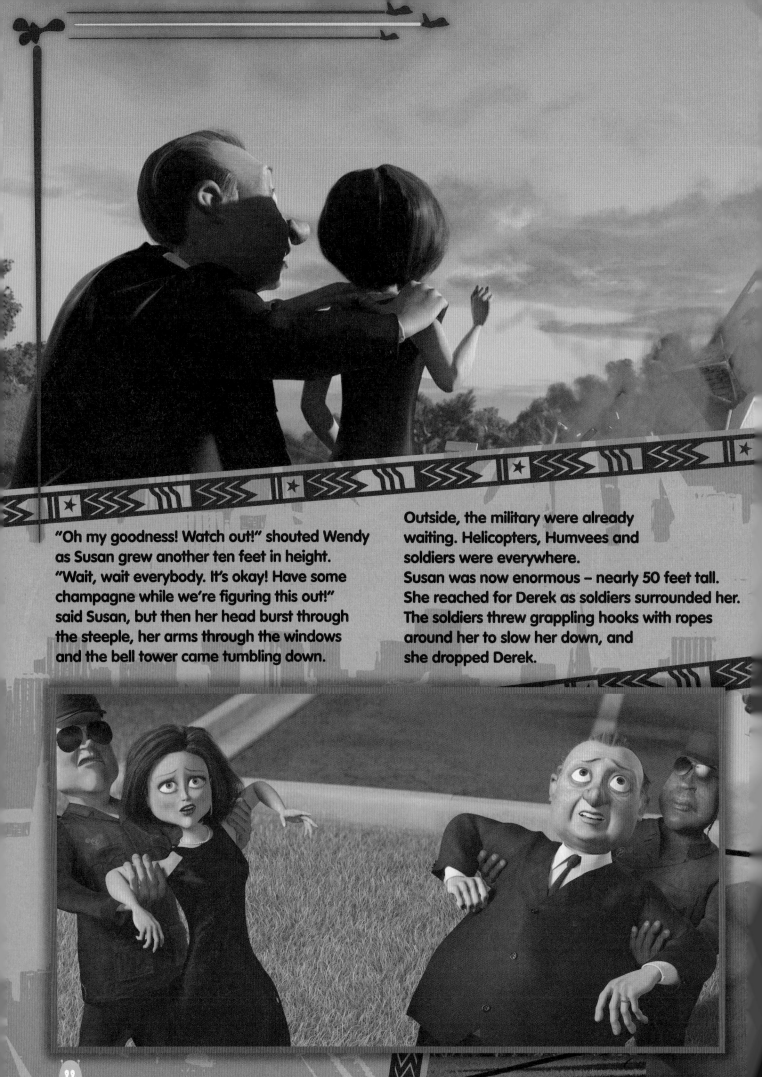

"Oh my goodness! Watch out!" shouted Wendy as Susan grew another ten feet in height. "Wait, wait everybody. It's okay! Have some champagne while we're figuring this out!" said Susan, but then her head burst through the steeple, her arms through the windows and the bell tower came tumbling down.

Outside, the military were already waiting. Helicopters, Humvees and soldiers were everywhere.
Susan was now enormous – nearly 50 feet tall. She reached for Derek as soldiers surrounded her. The soldiers threw grappling hooks with ropes around her to slow her down, and she dropped Derek.

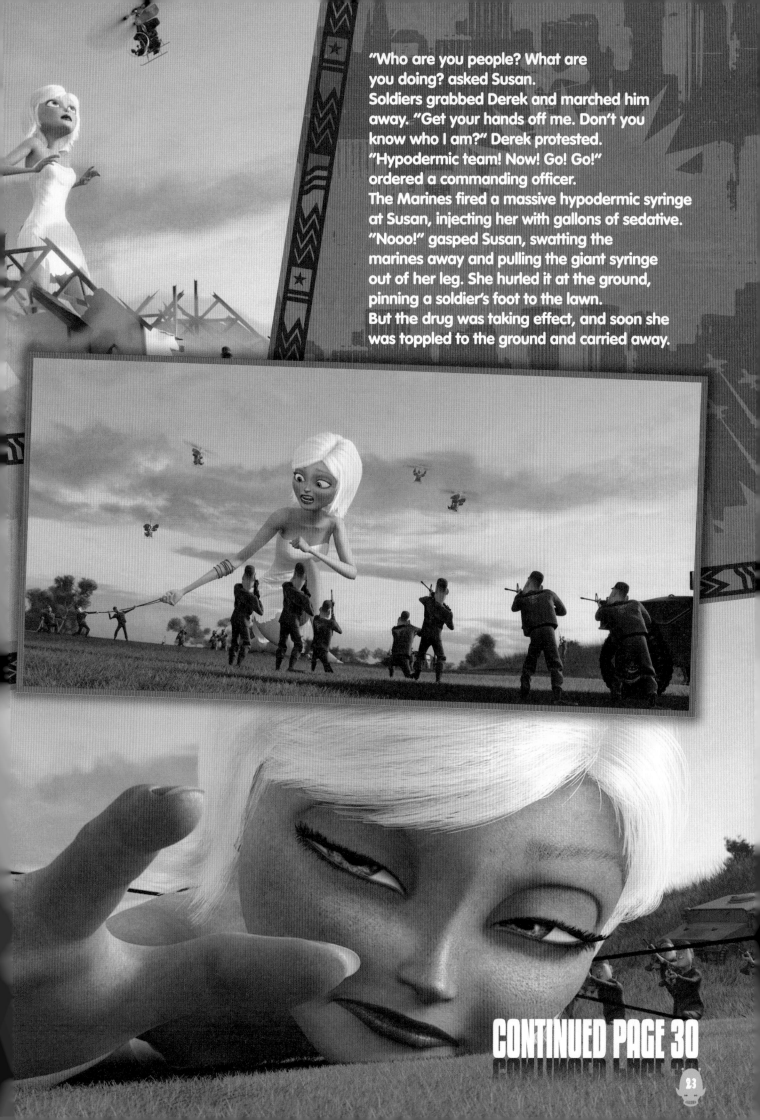

"Who are you people? What are you doing? asked Susan.
Soldiers grabbed Derek and marched him away. "Get your hands off me. Don't you know who I am?" Derek protested.
"Hypodermic team! Now! Go! Go!" ordered a commanding officer.
The Marines fired a massive hypodermic syringe at Susan, injecting her with gallons of sedative.
"Nooo!" gasped Susan, swatting the marines away and pulling the giant syringe out of her leg. She hurled it at the ground, pinning a soldier's foot to the lawn.
But the drug was taking effect, and soon she was toppled to the ground and carried away.

CONTINUED PAGE 30

23

TEST OF CHARACTER

Hidden in the grid are the names of eight characters from the film, reading up, down, across and diagonally, forward and backwards.

S	A	N	F	T	E	N	T	D	O	H	E	E	E
U	S	U	P	R	O	L	L	E	A	C	A	N	N
S	A	R	O	A	C	O	B	A	N	T	O	D	O
A	T	E	U	S	H	C	O	C	O	H	A	A	R
N	O	G	R	A	H	X	A	L	L	A	G	R	A
B	O	N	A	I	S	H	T	I	L	W	O	L	K
A	B	O	T	L	B	O	B	N	O	A	L	K	K
S	I	M	I	S	S	R	T	E	A	Y	E	O	A
A	L	L	O	N	E	E	R	C	R	R	O	S	S
P	L	I	R	T	S	T	O	A	E	A	B	I	I
C	H	A	S	H	A	E	A	D	R	S	O	K	K
B	O	N	O	R	O	N	C	A	N	I	N	N	N
C	O	E	L	E	E	S	A	F	A	B	A	I	I
M	L	D	L	D	L	E	L	O	L	A	B	L	L

- ○ Susan
- ○ Insectosaurus
- ○ Gallaxhar
- ○ Monger
- ○ Monster
- ○ Derek
- ○ Link
- ○ BOB

FOLLOW THE TRAIL

Who has found Susan? Is it Dr. Cockroach, The Missing Link, The Robot or B.O.B.?

MAKE ME A MONSTER

If you could be a monster, what sort would you be?

Answer the questions on this page and then draw and colour in a picture of how you would look if you were transformed into a monster.

If you had special powers, what would they be?

What would your monster name be?

Would you be big and scary with lots of teeth, or furry, funny and popular?

What would your mission be?

What group of people would be your main enemies?

What would be your main food?

What would you do to grown-ups who refused to obey your instructions?

What would be the first thing you would do when you ruled the universe?

A25 31-5X

Draw and colour in how you would look, and sign off with your own special monster signature or symbol.

ENCLOSURE

CATCHPHRASE QUIZ

Can you tell which of these characters matches up to which catchphrase? Draw a line connecting the speech bubble with its rightful owner.

Not only do I have an idea, I have a plan.

Allow me to explain in a way that your simple human mind can understand.

You wouldn't happen to have any uranium on you? I just need a smidge.

"It's a little hotter than I remember. Has the Earth gotten warmer?"

I may not have a brain, gentlemen, but I have an idea.

There probably isn't a jar in this world I can't open.

A2531-5X

Not sure about some of them? As you read through the stories in this annual, look back to this page when you come across a familiar catchphrase and you will be able to solve the puzzle.

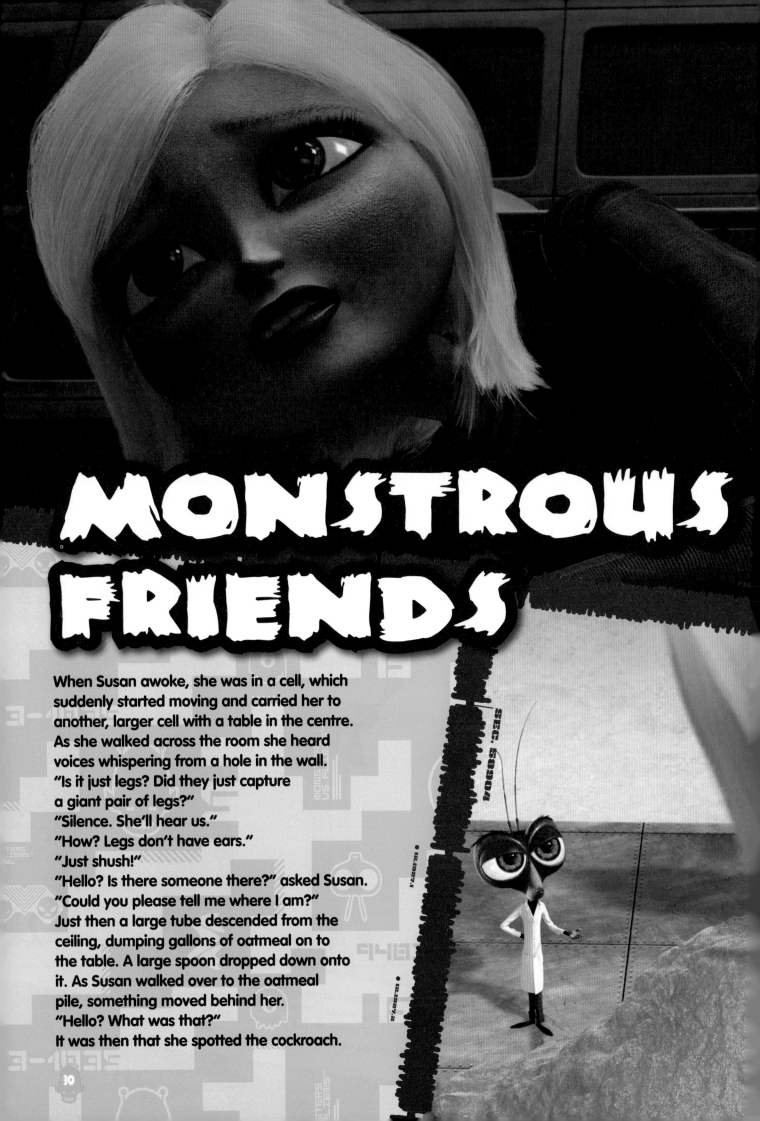

MONSTROUS FRIENDS

When Susan awoke, she was in a cell, which
suddenly started moving and carried her to
another, larger cell with a table in the centre.
As she walked across the room she heard
voices whispering from a hole in the wall.
"Is it just legs? Did they just capture
a giant pair of legs?"
"Silence. She'll hear us."
"How? Legs don't have ears."
"Just shush!"
"Hello? Is there someone there?" asked Susan.
"Could you please tell me where I am?"
Just then a large tube descended from the
ceiling, dumping gallons of oatmeal on to
the table. A large spoon dropped down onto
it. As Susan walked over to the oatmeal
pile, something moved behind her.
"Hello? What was that?"
It was then that she spotted the cockroach.

"Ewww!" cried
Susan, and she tried to swat
the cockroach with the giant spoon. It ducked
and dodged while waving its human hands at her.
"Will you stop…"
WHAM!
"Careful!"
WHAM!
"Please Madam!"
Susan kept slamming the spoon down.
"Stop… doing… that."
She stopped, finally.
"Whatever mad scientist made you, he
went all out," said Dr. Cockroach Ph.D.
"You can talk?" said Susan, dropping the spoon
and backing away from him, only to step
on something squishy. She reached down
and picked up a slimy looking object that
suddenly grew an eyeball and a mouth.
"Hi there!"

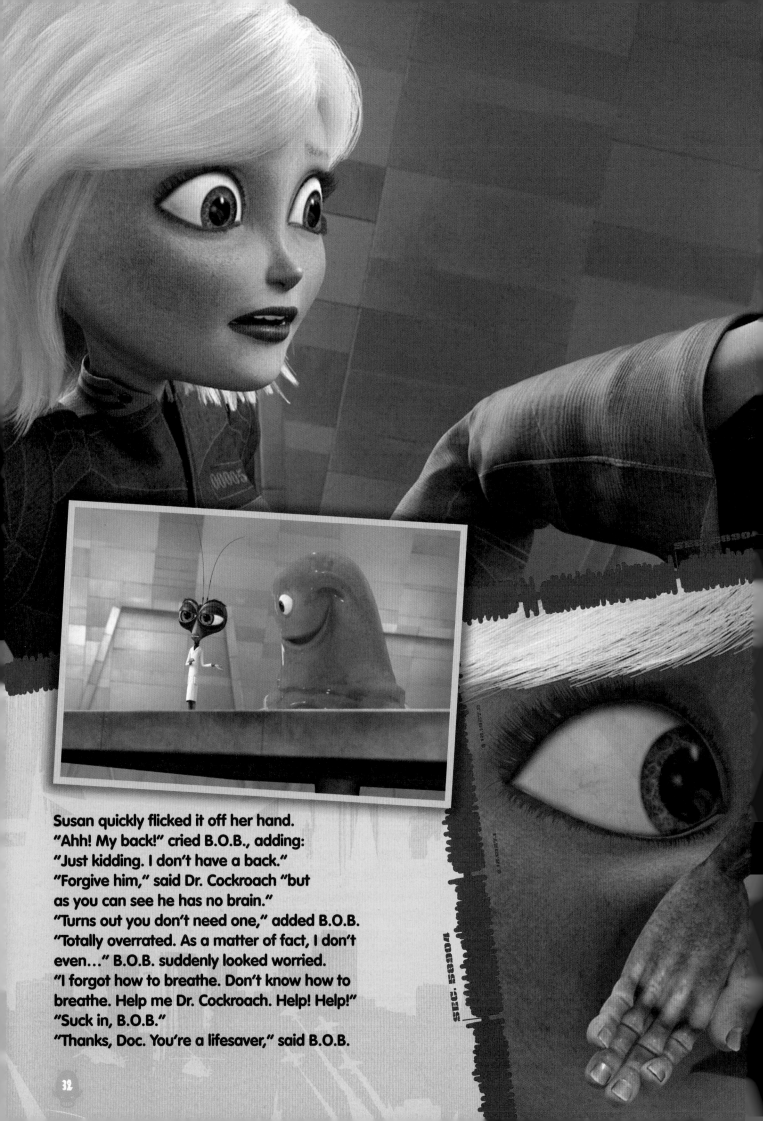

Susan quickly flicked it off her hand.

"Ahh! My back!" cried B.O.B., adding:
"Just kidding. I don't have a back."

"Forgive him," said Dr. Cockroach "but
as you can see he has no brain."

"Turns out you don't need one," added B.O.B.
"Totally overrated. As a matter of fact, I don't
even…" B.O.B. suddenly looked worried.

"I forgot how to breathe. Don't know how to
breathe. Help me Dr. Cockroach. Help! Help!"

"Suck in, B.O.B."

"Thanks, Doc. You're a lifesaver," said B.O.B.

Then Susan got her first glimpse of The Missing Link – he landed on top of her head and bent down to look her in the face! "Wow, look at you. I know what you're thinking. First day in prison, you wanna take down the toughest guy in the yard. Well, I'd like to see you try." He slid down her body and landed next to her foot, springing into a series of Kung Fu poses until he threw his back out. "Ninja – Ow. Ah, gosh," said The Missing Link. "Gentlemen, I'm afraid we are not making a very good first impression," said Dr. Cockroach.

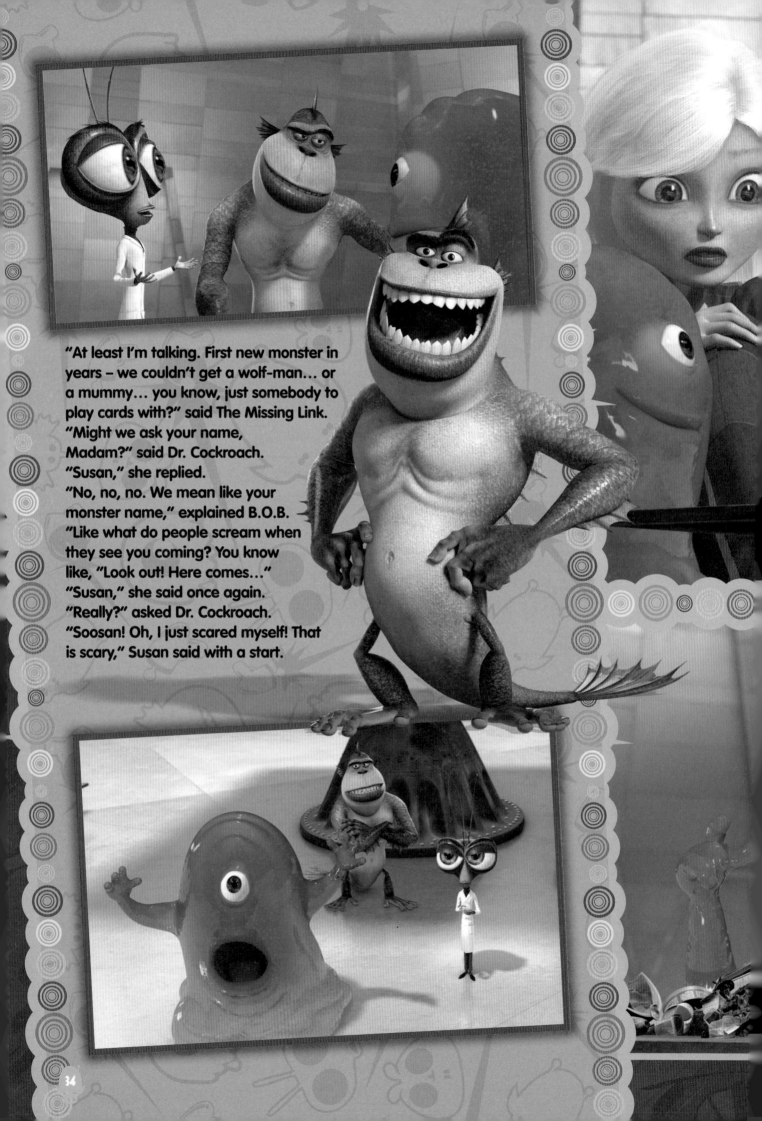

"At least I'm talking. First new monster in years – we couldn't get a wolf-man... or a mummy... you know, just somebody to play cards with?" said The Missing Link.

"Might we ask your name, Madam?" said Dr. Cockroach.

"Susan," she replied.

"No, no, no. We mean like your monster name," explained B.O.B. "Like what do people scream when they see you coming? You know like, "Look out! Here comes…""

"Susan," she said once again.

"Really?" asked Dr. Cockroach.

"Soosan! Oh, I just scared myself! That is scary," Susan said with a start.

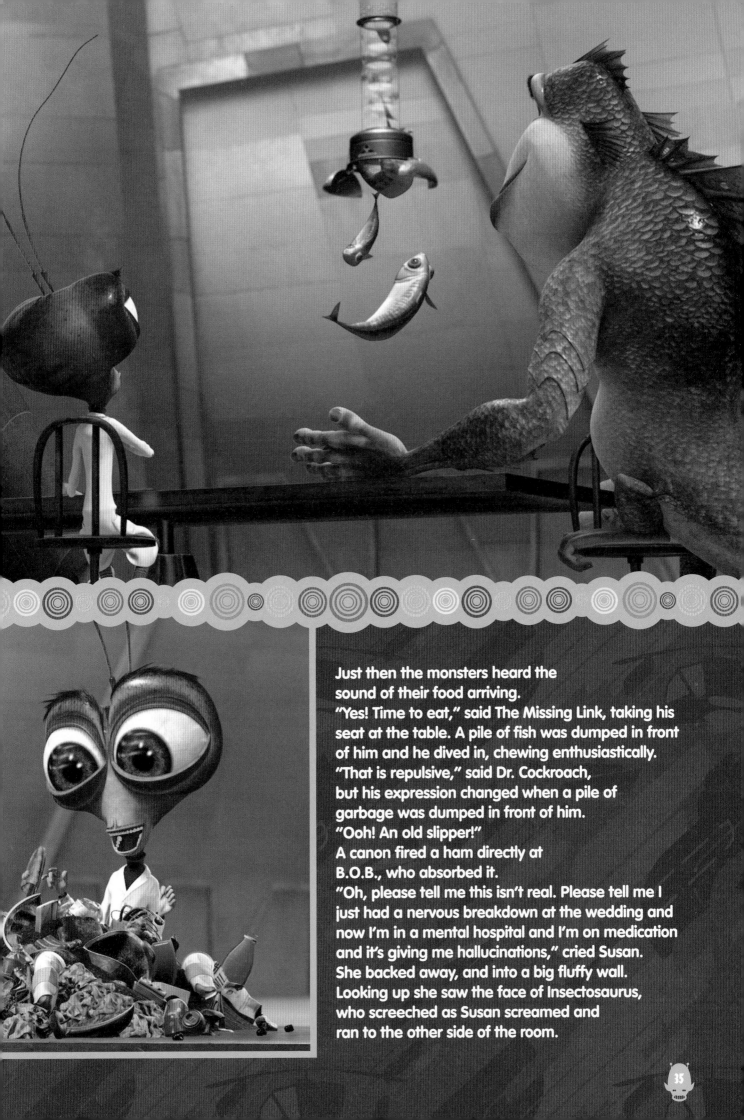

Just then the monsters heard the
sound of their food arriving.
"Yes! Time to eat," said The Missing Link, taking his
seat at the table. A pile of fish was dumped in front
of him and he dived in, chewing enthusiastically.
"That is repulsive," said Dr. Cockroach,
but his expression changed when a pile of
garbage was dumped in front of him.
"Ooh! An old slipper!"
A canon fired a ham directly at
B.O.B., who absorbed it.
"Oh, please tell me this isn't real. Please tell me I
just had a nervous breakdown at the wedding and
now I'm in a mental hospital and I'm on medication
and it's giving me hallucinations," cried Susan.
She backed away, and into a big fluffy wall.
Looking up she saw the face of Insectosaurus,
who screeched as Susan screamed and
ran to the other side of the room.

"A cyborg?" offered General Monger.
"Oh, no! You're a cyborg!" Susan cried.
"Madam I assure you I am not a cyborg.
The name is General W.R. Monger. I'm
in charge of this facility. Now follow me.
It is time for your orientation." Monger
jetted out of the door followed by Susan.

A large door opened and General
W.R. Monger flew in on a jet pack.
"Monsters, get back in your
cells!" he ordered
As they left, B.O.B. absorbed all of the
leftover food as he passed the table.
"Oh, thank goodness, a real person,"
said Susan. "You are a real person,
right? You're not one of those half-
person, half machine... you know.
What ever you call those things?"

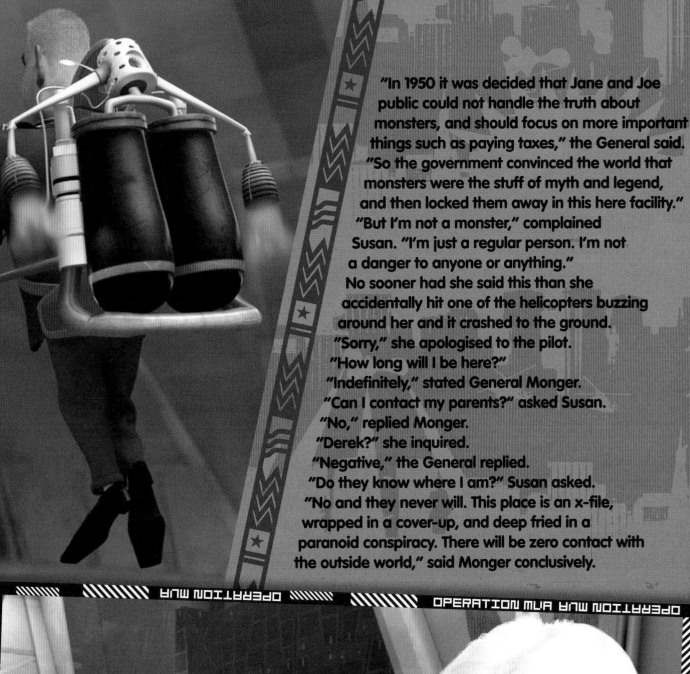

"In 1950 it was decided that Jane and Joe public could not handle the truth about monsters, and should focus on more important things such as paying taxes," the General said. "So the government convinced the world that monsters were the stuff of myth and legend, and then locked them away in this here facility."

"But I'm not a monster," complained Susan. "I'm just a regular person. I'm not a danger to anyone or anything."

No sooner had she said this than she accidentally hit one of the helicopters buzzing around her and it crashed to the ground.

"Sorry," she apologised to the pilot.

"How long will I be here?"

"Indefinitely," stated General Monger.

"Can I contact my parents?" asked Susan.

"No," replied Monger.

"Derek?" she inquired.

"Negative," the General replied.

"Do they know where I am?" Susan asked.

"No and they never will. This place is an x-file, wrapped in a cover-up, and deep fried in a paranoid conspiracy. There will be zero contact with the outside world," said Monger conclusively.

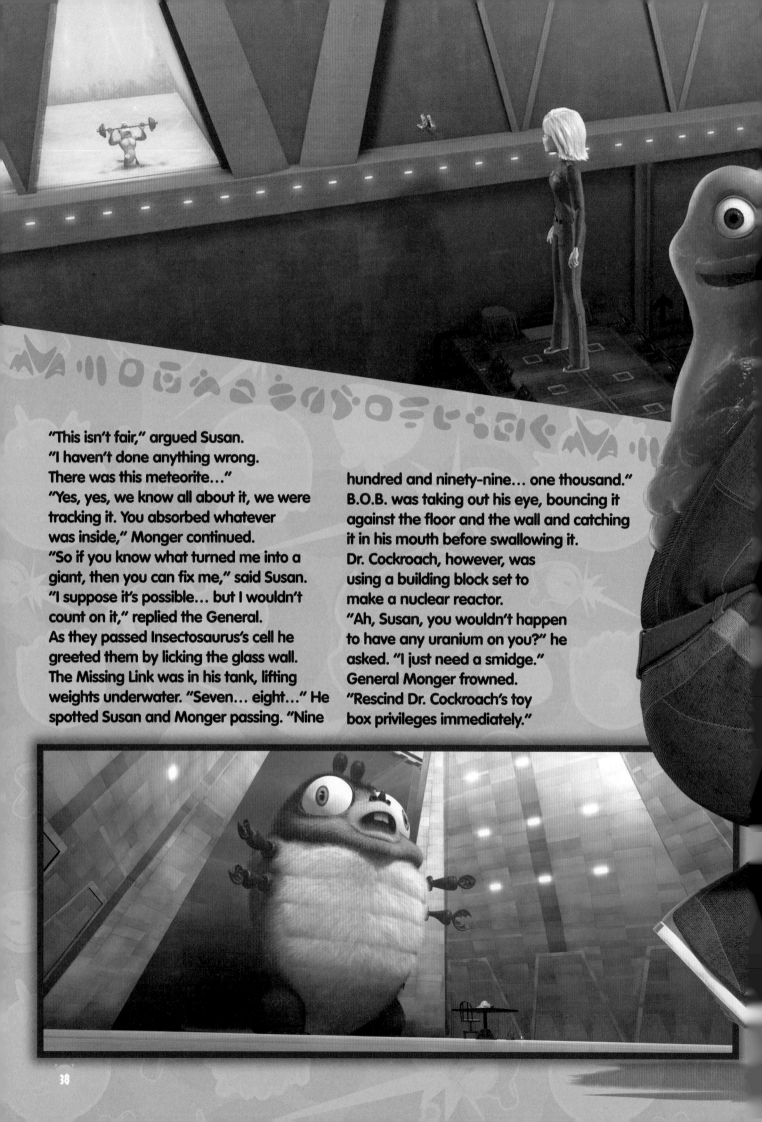

"This isn't fair," argued Susan. "I haven't done anything wrong. There was this meteorite…"

"Yes, yes, we know all about it, we were tracking it. You absorbed whatever was inside," Monger continued.

"So if you know what turned me into a giant, then you can fix me," said Susan.

"I suppose it's possible… but I wouldn't count on it," replied the General.

As they passed Insectosaurus's cell he greeted them by licking the glass wall. The Missing Link was in his tank, lifting weights underwater. "Seven… eight…" He spotted Susan and Monger passing. "Nine hundred and ninety-nine… one thousand." B.O.B. was taking out his eye, bouncing it against the floor and the wall and catching it in his mouth before swallowing it. Dr. Cockroach, however, was using a building block set to make a nuclear reactor.

"Ah, Susan, you wouldn't happen to have any uranium on you?" he asked. "I just need a smidge."

General Monger frowned.

"Rescind Dr. Cockroach's toy box privileges immediately."

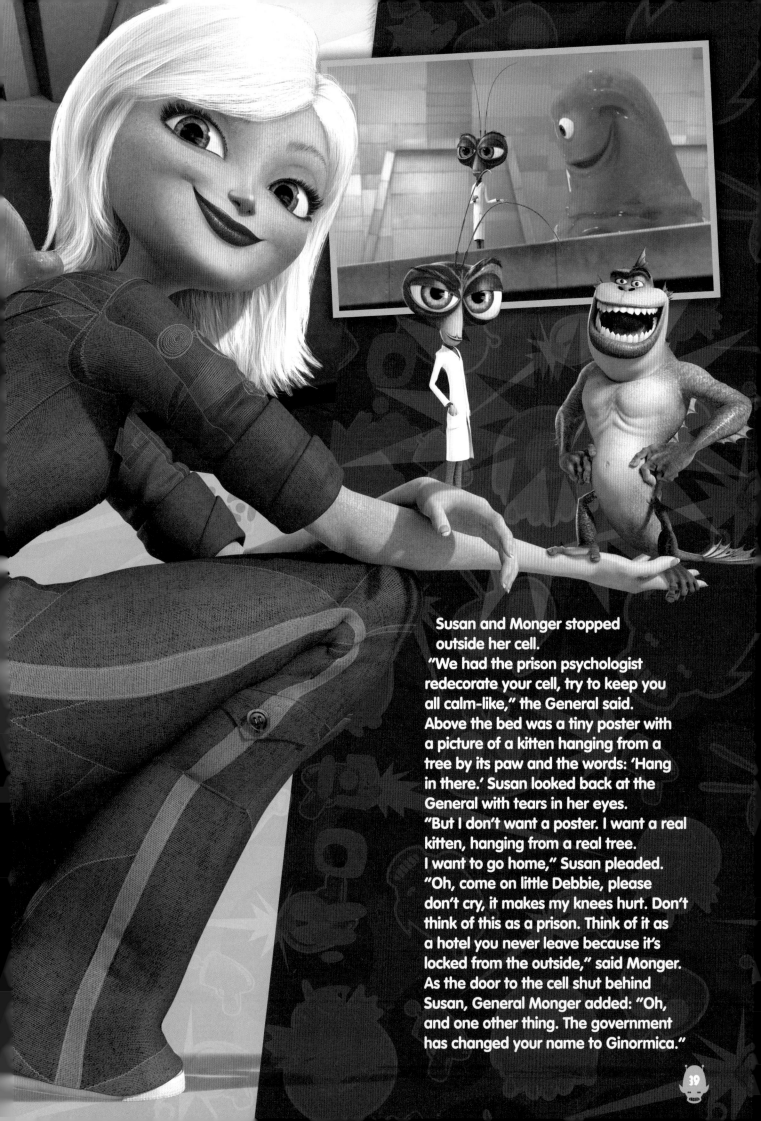

Susan and Monger stopped
outside her cell.

"We had the prison psychologist
redecorate your cell, try to keep you
all calm-like," the General said.
Above the bed was a tiny poster with
a picture of a kitten hanging from a
tree by its paw and the words: 'Hang
in there.' Susan looked back at the
General with tears in her eyes.

"But I don't want a poster. I want a real
kitten, hanging from a real tree.
I want to go home," Susan pleaded.

"Oh, come on little Debbie, please
don't cry, it makes my knees hurt. Don't
think of this as a prison. Think of it as
a hotel you never leave because it's
locked from the outside," said Monger.
As the door to the cell shut behind
Susan, General Monger added: "Oh,
and one other thing. The government
has changed your name to Ginormica."

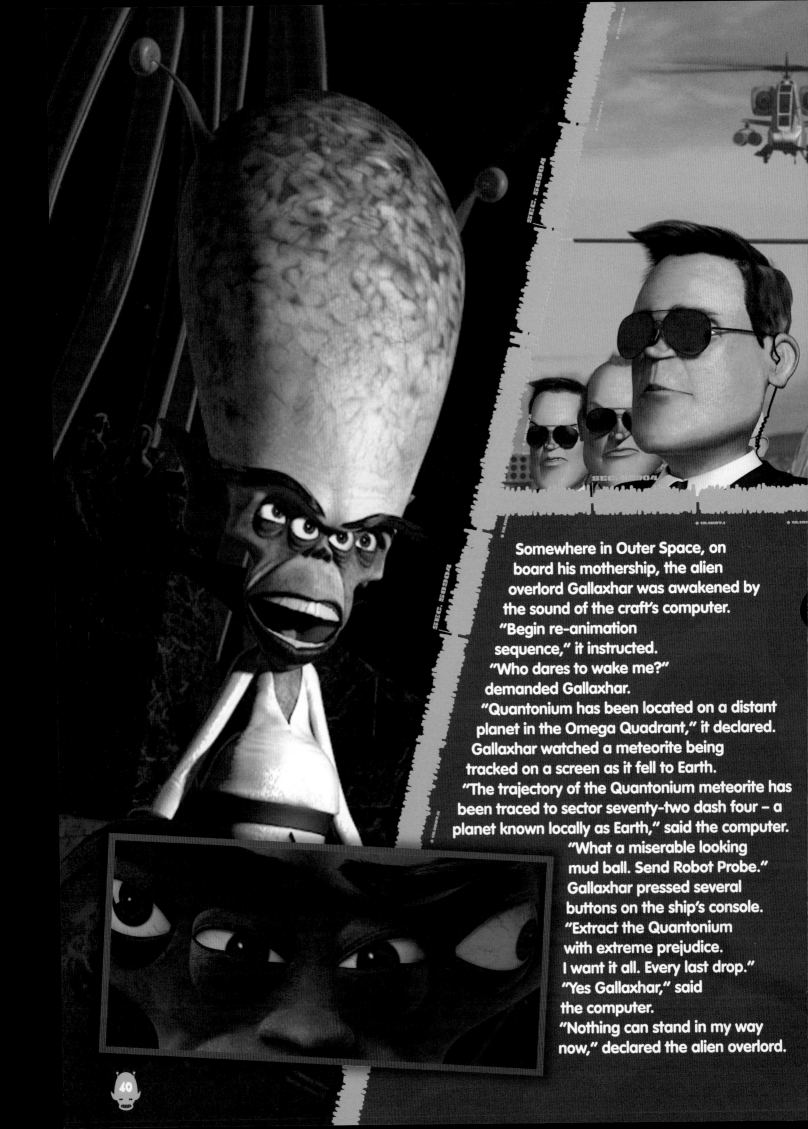

Somewhere in Outer Space, on board his mothership, the alien overlord Gallaxhar was awakened by the sound of the craft's computer.

"Begin re-animation sequence," it instructed.

"Who dares to wake me?" demanded Gallaxhar.

"Quantonium has been located on a distant planet in the Omega Quadrant," it declared. Gallaxhar watched a meteorite being tracked on a screen as it fell to Earth.

"The trajectory of the Quantonium meteorite has been traced to sector seventy-two dash four – a planet known locally as Earth," said the computer.

"What a miserable looking mud ball. Send Robot Probe." Gallaxhar pressed several buttons on the ship's console.

"Extract the Quantonium with extreme prejudice. I want it all. Every last drop."

"Yes Gallaxhar," said the computer.

"Nothing can stand in my way now," declared the alien overlord.

President Hathaway climbed the tall staircase that had been wheeled up to the Robot Probe, pausing part way up for a drink of water and to mop his brow. At the top he was at eye level with the alien robot. In front of him on the staircase was a music keyboard. He tapped out a friendly tune, but got no reaction.

Suddenly a large claw extended towards him as if it were about to offer a greeting, but stopped short and came down suddenly, smashing the keyboard. President Hathaway raced down the staircase as the robot began to advance.

He barked an order to his troops and a wave of bullets, rockets and missiles were fired at the robot, without any effect. "Full retreat! Full retreat! All troops!" barked a commanding officer. The President's Secret Service agents surrounded him to provide protection. He pulled out a revolver and pointed it at the robot.

"So that's how you want to play it? Eat lead, alien robot!" he yelled, firing wildly to no effect.

"Evidently they eat lead," he observed, as he headed for the safety of the Presidential helicopter.

In the war room, the President's military advisors gathered round a long table.
"Listen up," he declared. "I'm not going to go down in history as the President who was in office when the world came to an end so somebody think of something and think of it fast."
Just then the entrance door swooshed open and General Monger appeared on the balcony above them.
"Mr President, not only do I have an idea… but I have a plan!" he cried. Vaulting over the rail he parachuted down and landed in front of President Hathaway.

"Over the past fifty years I have captured monsters on the rampage and locked them up in a secret prison facility," Monger announced. A video of the monsters began running on a giant screen. "Mr President, say hello to Insectosaurus, The Missing Link, Dr. Cockroach Ph.D., B.O.B., and our latest addition, Ginormica." He turned to the President. "Sir, these monsters are our best and only chance to defeat that robot." One of the President's advisors piped up: "Don't we already have an alien problem, General? I don't think we need a monster problem, too." General Monger rounded on him. "You got a better idea, nerd?" "Okay, General," President Hathaway told him. "I propose we go forward with your monsters versus aliens idea thing-y."

CONTINUED PAGE 52

43

CHOCOLATE METEORITES

Use this recipe to make a really yummy snack that's out of this world, and bring your hunger crashing back down to earth with these crunchy treats.

INGREDIENTS

(makes 12 meteorites)

- 50 gr (2 oz) butter
- 50 gr (2 oz) caster sugar
- 3 tablespoons of Golden Syrup
- 50 gr (2 oz) sultanas or raisins
- 50 gr (2 oz) corn flakes
- 115 gr (4.06 oz) plain chocolate

○ Ask an adult to warm the butter, sugar and syrup in a saucepan over a low heat, stirring occasionally until the sugar has dissolved.

○ Stir in the fruit and corn flakes and allow to cool slightly.

○ Break up the chocolate and stir it in until it has melted.

○ Place heaped teaspoons of the mixture into paper cake cups.

○ Put in the fridge on a tray until firm.

WOBBLY B.O.B.S

B.O.B. will eat almost anything, but he's particularly fond of jelly. Have a go at making your own mini B.O.B. at home.

O Break the jelly into squares and place in a heat-resistant measuring jug and get an adult to pour 100 ml of hot water from a kettle on top.

O Stir with a spoon to dissolve the jelly and make it up to a pint with cold water.

O Allow it to cool, then rinse a glass tumbler with cold water.

O Pour in the jelly and leave overnight in the fridge.

O Get an adult to run a knife around the inside of the glass to loosen the jelly before turning the glass upside down on a plate. Lift the glass clear.

O Find a light coloured Smartie and push it into the jelly to make B.O.B.'s eye, colouring in the pupil with black writing icing.

INGREDIENTS

■ 1 packet blackcurrant jelly
■ 1 pint water
■ 1 tube Smarties
■ 1 tube black writing icing (optional)

WARNING: CONTENTS MAY BE RADIOACTIVE

DR. COCKROACH'S BRAIN TEASER

Time yourself and then let them have a go.

Arrange these letters in reverse alphabetical order:

P D G H L S K R M T

How many seconds are there in 2.5 hours?

If you have one fewer apples than Brian, and Brian has half as many as Tim, who has seven more than you, how many apples do you have?

46

DR. COCKROACH'S BRAIN SCRAMBLE

Being a mad scientist, Dr. Cockroach is fond of questions that bend the brain but can't be answered.

Here are a few examples to try on your friends and render them speechless.

What begins when Outer Space comes to an end?

What came first, the chicken or the egg?

Why is there only one Monopolies Commission?

Why do you never see baby pigeons?

Who bought the first telephone, and whom did he think he would be ringing?

Why can you only get mince pies at Christmas?

If God made man, who made God?

If you dug a hole deep enough, would you come out in Australia?

If dolphins are so intelligent, how come one has never won Mastermind?

47

GINORMOUS JOB

You're gonna need plenty of ink to colour in someone as big as Ginormica, who's almost 50 ft tall.

48

NOT PRESIDENT AND CORRECT

The president needs a helping hand to bring him back to his full VIP status, and you're just the person to do it. Get busy with your pen, joining the dots, and he might even let you ride in his helicopter.

FOUR TO

One of the monsters knows the way to the main power core at the centre of the maze. Find out which one by cracking this maze so you can shut down the alien spaceship and foil Gallaxhar's plan to take over the world.

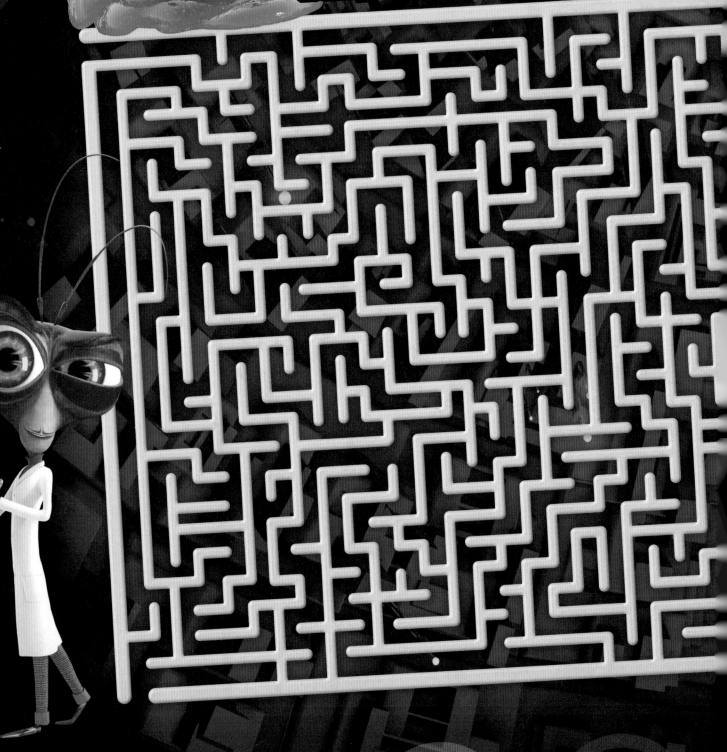

THE CORE

BATTLE OF THE BRIDGE

General Monger led the monsters out of the prison.

"So let me get this straight," said The Missing Link. "You want us to fight an alien robot?"

"And in exchange the President of these United States has authorised me to grant you your freedom," Monger replied.

Everyone's eyes went wide with excitement, including Susan's.

"I can't believe it – soon I'll be back in Derek's arms." She glanced down at her giant arms. "Or he'll be in mine."

"I can't wait for Spring break in Coco Beach, just freaking everybody out," dreamed The Missing Link.

"And I'll go back to my lab and finally finish my experiments," said Dr. Cockroach.

They were flown by transporter plane to San Francisco, arriving as the National Guard evacuated the city.

"Ah, feel the wind on your antennae," said Dr. Cockroach.

"I haven't been outside in fifty years. It's… it's amazing out here!" enthused B.O.B.

"It's a little hotter than I remember. Has the Earth gotten warmer? That would be great to know. That would be a very convenient truth," added B.O.B.

Just then the frightening sound of the robot's footsteps could be heard and they saw it appear through the fog.

"Hoo-wee! Now that's a robot!" declared General Monger. "It's huge," agreed Susan. "Try not to damage it too much, monsters. I might want to bring it back to the farm!" joked the General, heading back to the plane. "No, no, no! Wait!" yelled Susan. "You didn't say anything about it being huge!"

But the plane carried the General away, leaving the monsters to face their foe. "I think he's seen us," said B.O.B. "Hello! Hi! How you doin'? Welcome. We are here to destroy you." "I can't fight that thing!"

complained Susan. "I'm hyperventilating! Does anybody have a giant paper bag?"

"Re-lax. Old Link's got this under control," said The Missing Link "Hide in the city, Susan. You'll be safe there."

Susan set off, running towards the city while The Missing Link prepared for a fight.

"Finally some action! I'm going to turn that oversized tin can into a really dented oversized tin can!" he said.

The robot marched towards them and Dr. Cockroach and The Missing Link dived out of the way of its giant foot, which landed directly on B.O.B. As it lifted its foot, B.O.B. was stuck to the bottom.

"I got him you guys!" yelled B.O.B. "I got him! Don't worry I won't let go! I'm wearing him down. Please tell me he's slowing down!"

As the robot headed for the city, Dr. Cockroach spotted a trolley car on the back of a truck.

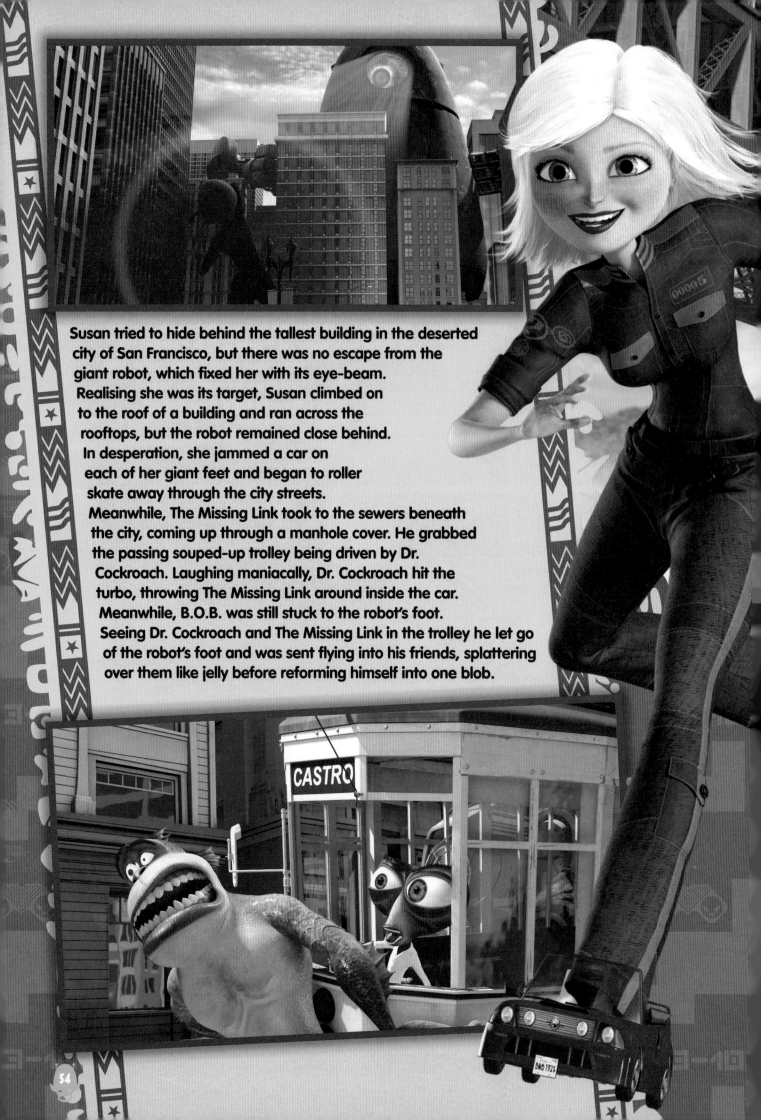

Susan tried to hide behind the tallest building in the deserted city of San Francisco, but there was no escape from the giant robot, which fixed her with its eye-beam. Realising she was its target, Susan climbed on to the roof of a building and ran across the rooftops, but the robot remained close behind. In desperation, she jammed a car on each of her giant feet and began to roller skate away through the city streets.

Meanwhile, The Missing Link took to the sewers beneath the city, coming up through a manhole cover. He grabbed the passing souped-up trolley being driven by Dr. Cockroach. Laughing maniacally, Dr. Cockroach hit the turbo, throwing The Missing Link around inside the car. Meanwhile, B.O.B. was still stuck to the robot's foot. Seeing Dr. Cockroach and The Missing Link in the trolley he let go of the robot's foot and was sent flying into his friends, splattering over them like jelly before reforming himself into one blob.

CASTRO

Susan had reached the city's famous Golden Gate Bridge, swerving in and out of the vehicles on the road.

An oil tanker flipped over as the driver caught sight of Susan in his mirror, trapping a car beneath it. As Susan stopped to help, she caught sight of the robot approaching.

Drivers screamed as the robot reached the bridge. It tried to grab Susan but missed, hitting the bridge with a hard jolt instead. Cables supporting the bridge snapped, cars and broken bits of the bridge slid down towards the water far below. The Missing Link, Dr. Cockroach and B.O.B. weaved their way through the traffic to reach Susan. "Excuse me, it's trying to kill me. Why is it doing that? Why would

it..." cried Susan as the robot grabbed her with its crab-like metal claw. But Susan's super strength enabled her to hold the claw open and escape.

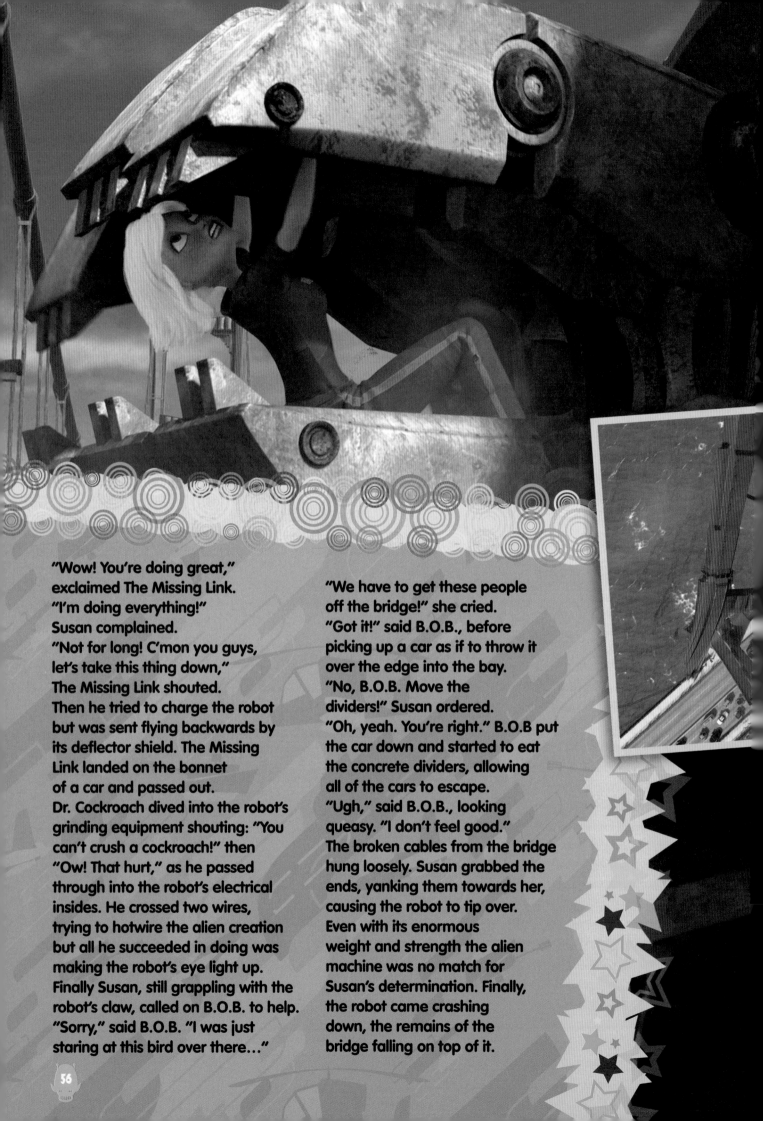

"Wow! You're doing great," exclaimed The Missing Link. "I'm doing everything!" Susan complained.

"Not for long! C'mon you guys, let's take this thing down," The Missing Link shouted. Then he tried to charge the robot but was sent flying backwards by its deflector shield. The Missing Link landed on the bonnet of a car and passed out.

Dr. Cockroach dived into the robot's grinding equipment shouting: "You can't crush a cockroach!" then "Ow! That hurt," as he passed through into the robot's electrical insides. He crossed two wires, trying to hotwire the alien creation but all he succeeded in doing was making the robot's eye light up. Finally Susan, still grappling with the robot's claw, called on B.O.B. to help. "Sorry," said B.O.B. "I was just staring at this bird over there..."

"We have to get these people off the bridge!" she cried. "Got it!" said B.O.B., before picking up a car as if to throw it over the edge into the bay. "No, B.O.B. Move the dividers!" Susan ordered. "Oh, yeah. You're right." B.O.B put the car down and started to eat the concrete dividers, allowing all of the cars to escape. "Ugh," said B.O.B., looking queasy. "I don't feel good." The broken cables from the bridge hung loosely. Susan grabbed the ends, yanking them towards her, causing the robot to tip over. Even with its enormous weight and strength the alien machine was no match for Susan's determination. Finally, the robot came crashing down, the remains of the bridge falling on top of it.

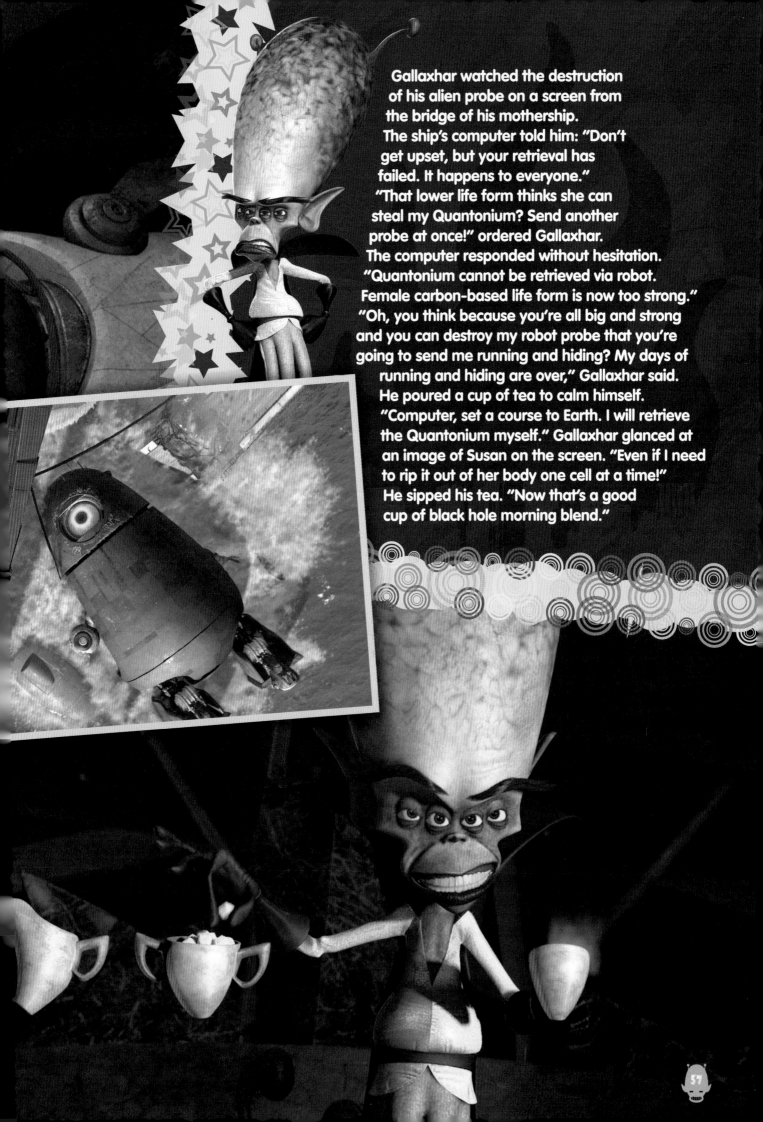

Gallaxhar watched the destruction of his alien probe on a screen from the bridge of his mothership.

The ship's computer told him: "Don't get upset, but your retrieval has failed. It happens to everyone."

"That lower life form thinks she can steal my Quantonium? Send another probe at once!" ordered Gallaxhar.

The computer responded without hesitation. "Quantonium cannot be retrieved via robot. Female carbon-based life form is now too strong."

"Oh, you think because you're all big and strong and you can destroy my robot probe that you're going to send me running and hiding? My days of running and hiding are over," Gallaxhar said.

He poured a cup of tea to calm himself. "Computer, set a course to Earth. I will retrieve the Quantonium myself." Gallaxhar glanced at an image of Susan on the screen. "Even if I need to rip it out of her body one cell at a time!" He sipped his tea. "Now that's a good cup of black hole morning blend."

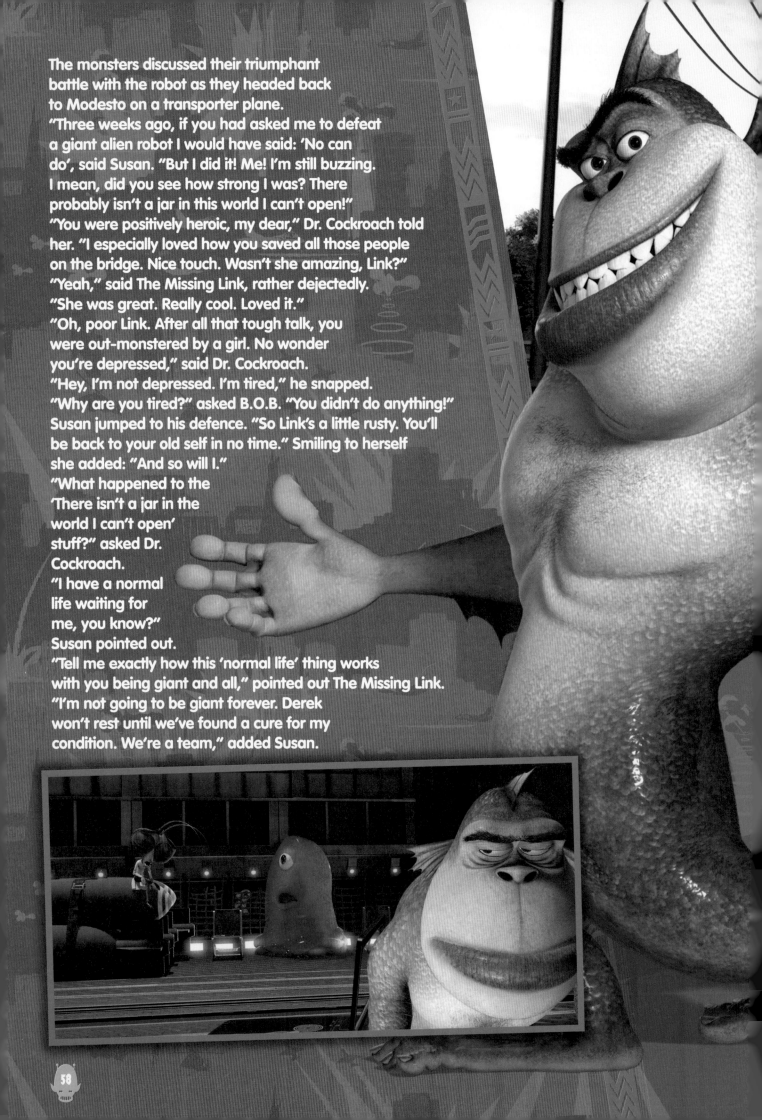

The monsters discussed their triumphant battle with the robot as they headed back to Modesto on a transporter plane.

"Three weeks ago, if you had asked me to defeat a giant alien robot I would have said: 'No can do', said Susan. "But I did it! Me! I'm still buzzing. I mean, did you see how strong I was? There probably isn't a jar in this world I can't open!"

"You were positively heroic, my dear," Dr. Cockroach told her. "I especially loved how you saved all those people on the bridge. Nice touch. Wasn't she amazing, Link?"

"Yeah," said The Missing Link, rather dejectedly. "She was great. Really cool. Loved it."

"Oh, poor Link. After all that tough talk, you were out-monstered by a girl. No wonder you're depressed," said Dr. Cockroach.

"Hey, I'm not depressed. I'm tired," he snapped.

"Why are you tired?" asked B.O.B. "You didn't do anything!"

Susan jumped to his defence. "So Link's a little rusty. You'll be back to your old self in no time." Smiling to herself she added: "And so will I."

"What happened to the 'There isn't a jar in the world I can't open' stuff?" asked Dr. Cockroach.

"I have a normal life waiting for me, you know?" Susan pointed out.

"Tell me exactly how this 'normal life' thing works with you being giant and all," pointed out The Missing Link.

"I'm not going to be giant forever. Derek won't rest until we've found a cure for my condition. We're a team," added Susan.

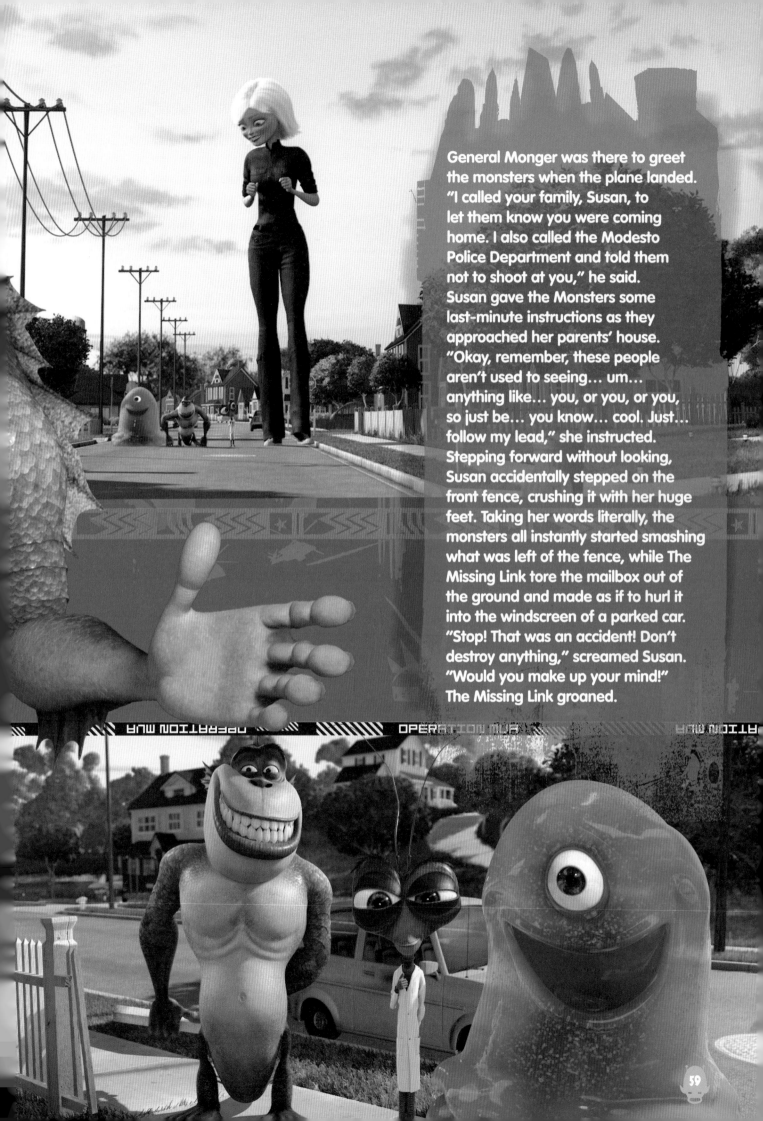

General Monger was there to greet the monsters when the plane landed. "I called your family, Susan, to let them know you were coming home. I also called the Modesto Police Department and told them not to shoot at you," he said. Susan gave the Monsters some last-minute instructions as they approached her parents' house. "Okay, remember, these people aren't used to seeing… um… anything like… you, or you, or you, so just be… you know… cool. Just… follow my lead," she instructed. Stepping forward without looking, Susan accidentally stepped on the front fence, crushing it with her huge feet. Taking her words literally, the monsters all instantly started smashing what was left of the fence, while The Missing Link tore the mailbox out of the ground and made as if to hurl it into the windscreen of a parked car. "Stop! That was an accident! Don't destroy anything," screamed Susan. "Would you make up your mind!" The Missing Link groaned.

Susan's parents rushed forward and each hugged one of her ankles.
"Mom? Daddy?" smiled Susan.
"Did they experiment on you?" asked her mother.
"No, Mom. I'm fine," replied Susan.
She noticed everyone's frightened expression as they caught sight of the monsters.
"It's okay, they're with me. These are my new friends," Susan exclaimed.
B.O.B. burst forward and hugged Susan's mother, her screams getting muffled by his jelly-like body.

"Oh, Derek, I missed you so much! Thinking that we'd someday be together again is the only thing that got me through prison. I love you! I love this man!" said B.O.B.
Susan intervened. "No, B.O.B. That's my mother! You're suffocating her."
He spat her out. Looking slimy and dishevelled, Susan's mother cried: "I tasted ham!"
"Sorry Mom. He's just a hugger." Susan looked around. "Where's Derek?"
"He's at work, sweetie," said her mother. Susan's father explained. "You know how he is about his career."
"Well, we're not gonna celebrate without him!" declared Susan, turning to go and find him.
"What do I do with... all your little friends?" asked her mother.
"Just put out some snacks. They'll eat anything," Susan confirmed.

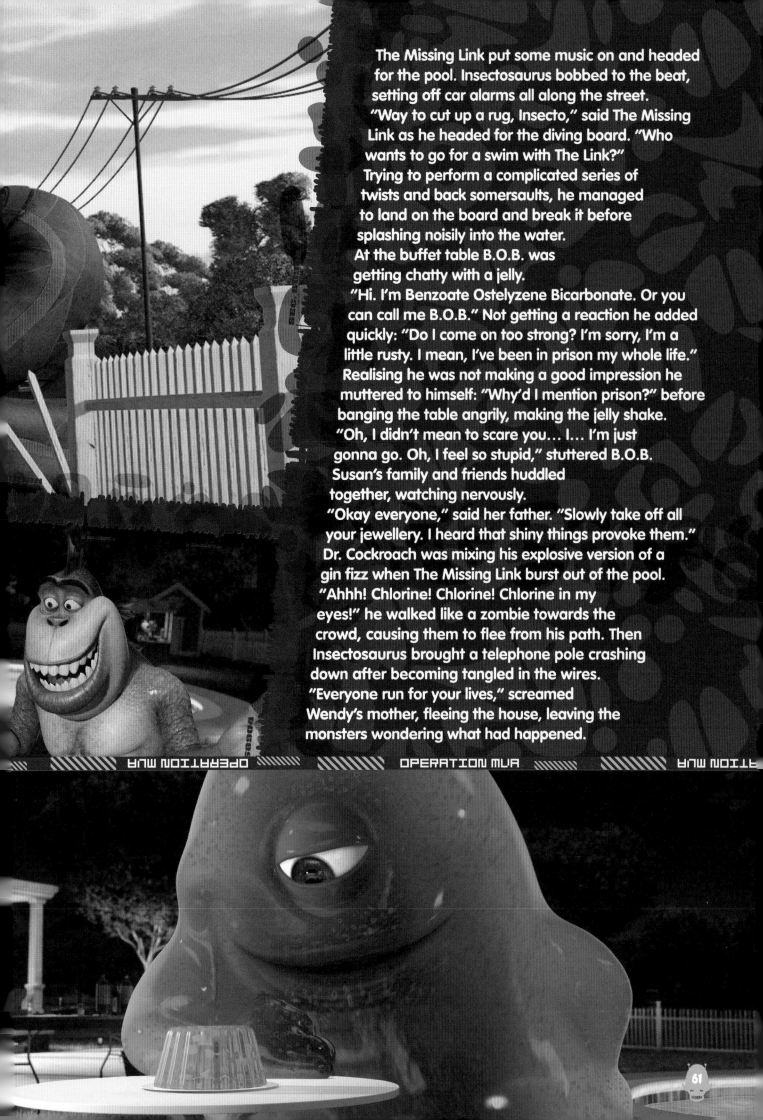

The Missing Link put some music on and headed for the pool. Insectosaurus bobbed to the beat, setting off car alarms all along the street.

"Way to cut up a rug, Insecto," said The Missing Link as he headed for the diving board. "Who wants to go for a swim with The Link?" Trying to perform a complicated series of twists and back somersaults, he managed to land on the board and break it before splashing noisily into the water.

At the buffet table B.O.B. was getting chatty with a jelly.

"Hi. I'm Benzoate Ostelyzene Bicarbonate. Or you can call me B.O.B." Not getting a reaction he added quickly: "Do I come on too strong? I'm sorry, I'm a little rusty. I mean, I've been in prison my whole life." Realising he was not making a good impression he muttered to himself: "Why'd I mention prison?" before banging the table angrily, making the jelly shake.

"Oh, I didn't mean to scare you... I... I'm just gonna go. Oh, I feel so stupid," stuttered B.O.B.

Susan's family and friends huddled together, watching nervously.

"Okay everyone," said her father. "Slowly take off all your jewellery. I heard that shiny things provoke them."

Dr. Cockroach was mixing his explosive version of a gin fizz when The Missing Link burst out of the pool.

"Ahhh! Chlorine! Chlorine! Chlorine in my eyes!" he walked like a zombie towards the crowd, causing them to flee from his path. Then Insectosaurus brought a telephone pole crashing down after becoming tangled in the wires.

"Everyone run for your lives," screamed Wendy's mother, fleeing the house, leaving the monsters wondering what had happened.

Derek had just finished his final weather bulletin on Channel 172 and the sound girl was removing his microphone when she screamed. Derek saw Susan peering through the window of the TV station building. She reached through and lifted him up, accidentally knocking his head against the window as she carried him out of the building. "Oh, Derek. You wouldn't believe my last three weeks. You just wouldn't believe it." Susan smothered him with a giant kiss. "Thinking about you was the only thing that kept me sane." Derek gasped for breath. "Can't breath, ribs collapsing."

"Oh, my gosh! Oh, my gosh I'm so sorry. On my God!" said Susan as she put him down on the station roof. "Is that better? Okay? Okay?"

"Yeah," Derek managed with a struggle.

"I'm just still kind of getting used to my new strength," she admitted.

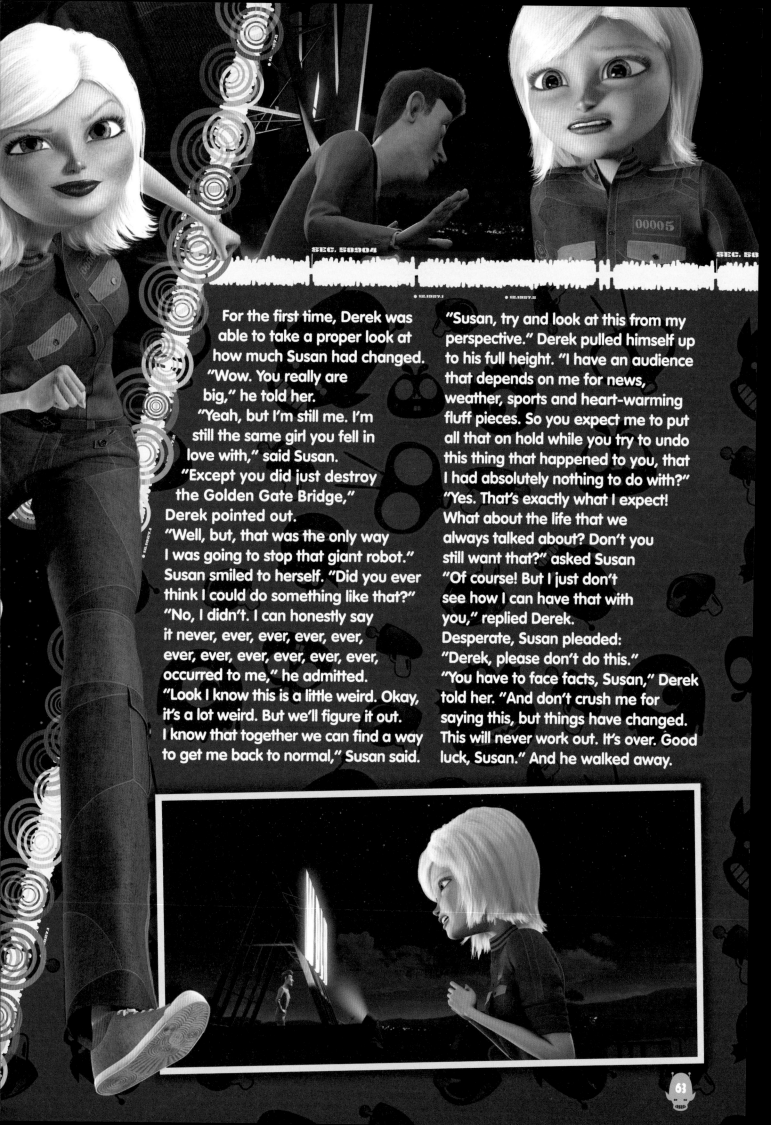

For the first time, Derek was able to take a proper look at how much Susan had changed. "Wow. You really are big," he told her.

"Yeah, but I'm still me. I'm still the same girl you fell in love with," said Susan.

"Except you did just destroy the Golden Gate Bridge," Derek pointed out.

"Well, but, that was the only way I was going to stop that giant robot." Susan smiled to herself. "Did you ever think I could do something like that?"

"No, I didn't. I can honestly say it never, ever, ever, ever, ever, ever, ever, ever, ever, ever, ever, occurred to me," he admitted.

"Look I know this is a little weird. Okay, it's a lot weird. But we'll figure it out. I know that together we can find a way to get me back to normal," Susan said.

"Susan, try and look at this from my perspective." Derek pulled himself up to his full height. "I have an audience that depends on me for news, weather, sports and heart-warming fluff pieces. So you expect me to put all that on hold while you try to undo this thing that happened to you, that I had absolutely nothing to do with?"

"Yes. That's exactly what I expect! What about the life that we always talked about? Don't you still want that?" asked Susan

"Of course! But I just don't see how I can have that with you," replied Derek.

Desperate, Susan pleaded: "Derek, please don't do this."

"You have to face facts, Susan," Derek told her. "And don't crush me for saying this, but things have changed. This will never work out. It's over. Good luck, Susan." And he walked away.

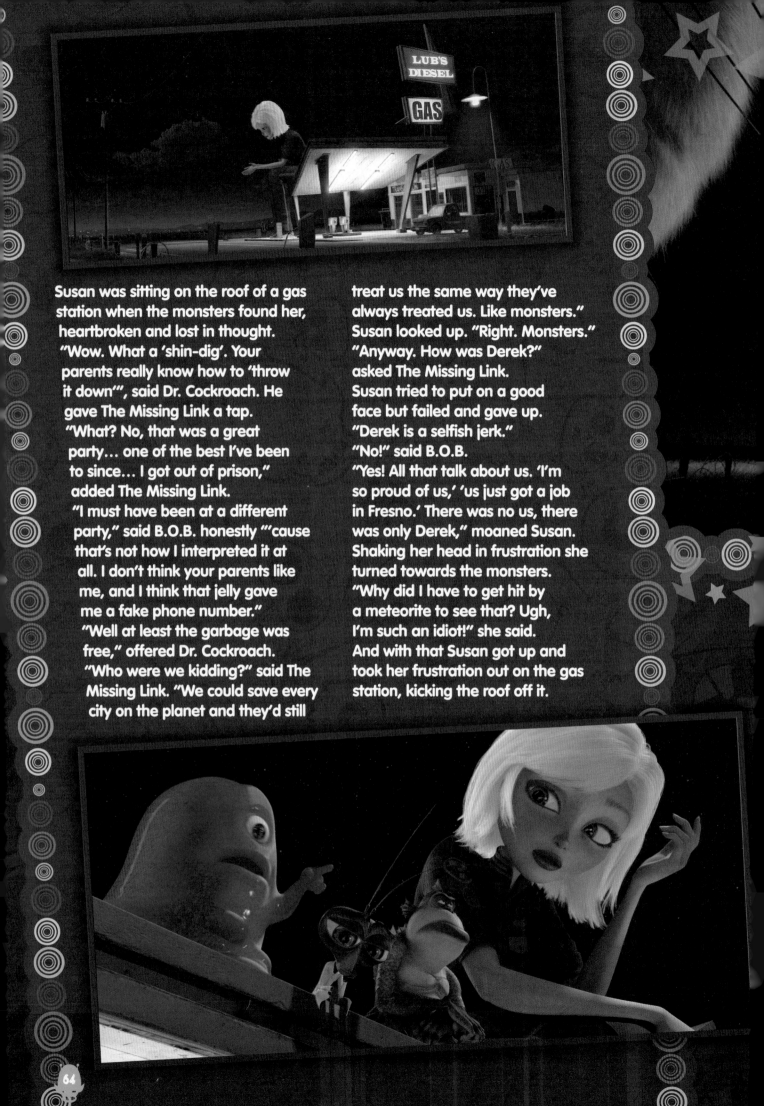

Susan was sitting on the roof of a gas station when the monsters found her, heartbroken and lost in thought.

"Wow. What a 'shin-dig'. Your parents really know how to 'throw it down'", said Dr. Cockroach. He gave The Missing Link a tap.

"What? No, that was a great party… one of the best I've been to since… I got out of prison," added The Missing Link.

"I must have been at a different party," said B.O.B. honestly "'cause that's not how I interpreted it at all. I don't think your parents like me, and I think that jelly gave me a fake phone number."

"Well at least the garbage was free," offered Dr. Cockroach.

"Who were we kidding?" said The Missing Link. "We could save every city on the planet and they'd still treat us the same way they've always treated us. Like monsters."

Susan looked up. "Right. Monsters."

"Anyway. How was Derek?" asked The Missing Link.

Susan tried to put on a good face but failed and gave up. "Derek is a selfish jerk."

"No!" said B.O.B.

"Yes! All that talk about us. 'I'm so proud of us,' 'us just got a job in Fresno.' There was no us, there was only Derek," moaned Susan. Shaking her head in frustration she turned towards the monsters. "Why did I have to get hit by a meteorite to see that? Ugh, I'm such an idiot!" she said. And with that Susan got up and took her frustration out on the gas station, kicking the roof off it.

"Why did I ever think life with Derek would be so amazing, anyway? I mean, look at all the stuff I've done without him. Fighting an alien robot! That was me, not him, and that was amazing." Susan knelt down to get closer to the monsters. "Meeting you guys? Amazing." She addressed each of them individually, pointing out their talents.

"Dr. Cockroach! You can crawl up walls and build a supercomputer out of a pizza box, two cans of hair spray and…"

"… a paperclip," he volunteered.

"Amazing! And you, Link. You hardly need an introduction. You're The Missing Link! You personally carried 250 co-eds off Coco Beach and still had the strength to fight off the National Guard."

"And the Coast Guard, and also the lifeguard," added The Missing Link.

"Amazing! B.O.B. Who else could fall from unimaginable heights and end up without a single scratch?"

"Link?" suggested B.O.B.

"You!" said Susan.

"Amazing!" said B.O.B.

The Missing Link turned to Susan.

"Susan, don't short change yourself."

"Oh, I'm not gonna short change myself ever again. And the name is Ginormica," Susan said firmly.

But she had hardly finished speaking when a beam of light from above enveloped her and she was whisked up into the air.

CONTINUED PAGE 72

65

BOARD GAME

1 START	**2**	**3**	**4** B.O.B shakes you up to 30	**5**	**6**	**7**
28	**27**	**26**	**25**	**24**	**23**	**22**
29	**30**	**31**	**32**	**33** Dr Cockroach's ideas take you to 49	**34**	**35** Galla stan your down
56	**55**	**54**	**53**	**52**	**51**	**50**
57	**58**	**59** Susan carries you to 74	**60**	**61**	**62**	**63**
84	**83**	**82**	**81**	**80** Gallaxhar's robot is in your way – bacl to 62	**79**	**78**
85	**86**	**87**	**88** Gallaxhar in your path means it's back to 71	**89**	**90**	**91**

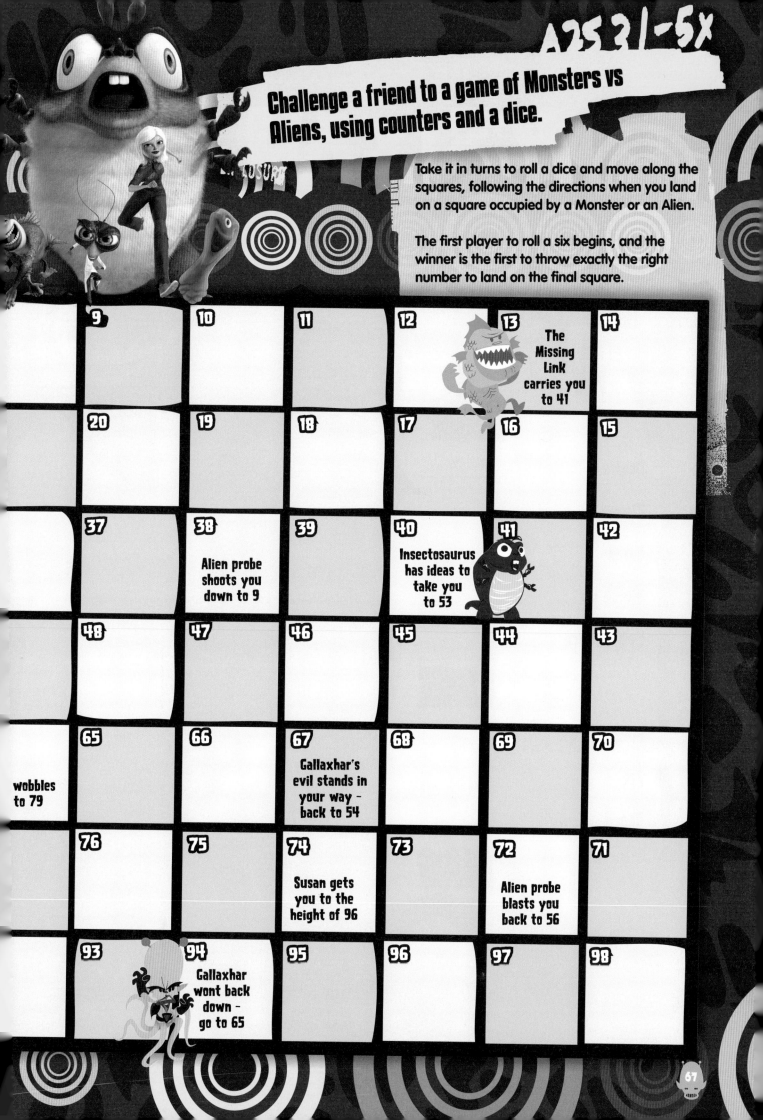

A2531-5X

Challenge a friend to a game of Monsters vs Aliens, using counters and a dice.

Take it in turns to roll a dice and move along the squares, following the directions when you land on a square occupied by a Monster or an Alien.

The first player to roll a six begins, and the winner is the first to throw exactly the right number to land on the final square.

9	10	11	12	13 The Missing Link carries you to 41	14
20	19	18	17	16	15
37	38 Alien probe shoots you down to 9	39	40 Insectosaurus has ideas to take you to 53	41	42
48	47	46	45	44	43
65	66	67 Gallaxhar's evil stands in your way – back to 54	68	69	70
76	75	74 Susan gets you to the height of 96	73	72 Alien probe blasts you back to 56	71
93	94 Gallaxhar wont back down – go to 65	95	96	97	98

wobbles to 79

LINK'S LEAP

Help The Missing Link make the leap from fish to man in ten stages by solving the clues that change one letter at a time.

FISH

Desire   wish

Clever   _____

Drink   _____

Winch up   _____

Eye closure   _____

LINK

Single stripe   _____

Pit   _____

Beard   _____

MAN

68

UNTANGLE SUSAN

Arrange all of the letters in the word 'Ginormica' in the spaces in each of these two puzzles to spell three words reading from left to right.

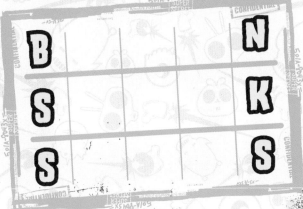

SOLVE THE RIDDLE

Your special mission has been delivered in code. Solve the clues to crack the riddle. Each clue will give you a letter towards a three-word answer. We'll tell you the first word has four letters, the second three and the third six.

- The first is in SAW but not in HOE.
- The second is in ARM but not in BOW.
- The third is in VET but not in TEN.
- The fourth is in AXE and also in PEN.
- The fifth is in ART and also in RAT.
- The sixth is in HIP and also in HAT.
- The seventh is in TEA but not in LIP.
- The eighth is in APE and also in TIP.
- The ninth is in OLD and also in LID.
- The tenth is in BAD but not in BID.
- The eleventh is in ANT and also in TAN.
- The twelfth is in MEN but not in MAN.
- My last is in PIT and also in PAT.

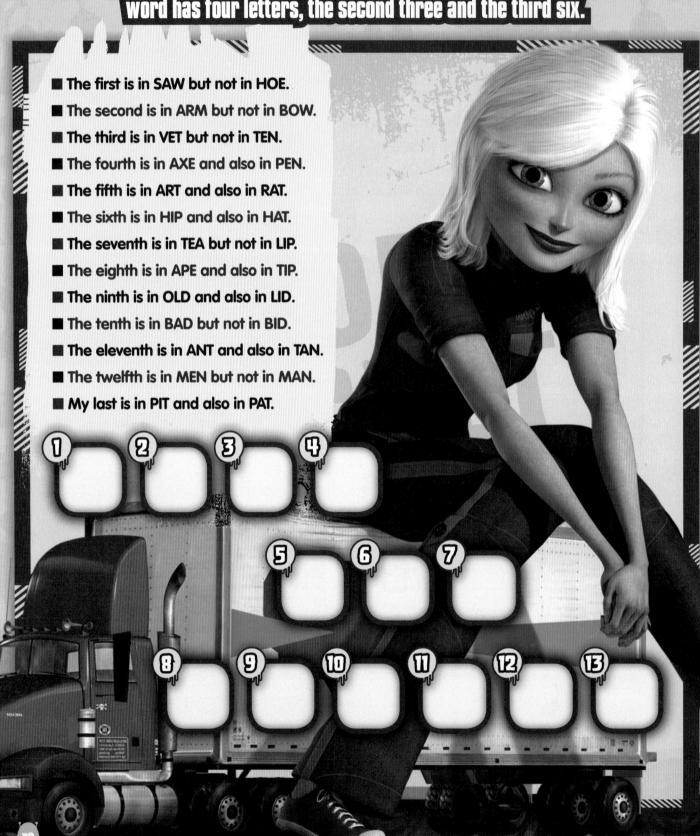

1 2 3 4
5 6 7
8 9 10 11 12 13

DR. COCKROACH'S ODD BOD

Four of these pictures can be grouped into pairs, leaving one as the odd one out, but which go with which?

a

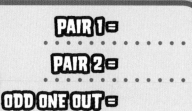
783-565—

b

783-565—

PAIR 1 = ...
PAIR 2 = ...
ODD ONE OUT = ...

c

783-565—

d

783-565—

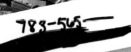

e

783-565—

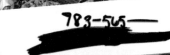

71

SPACESHIP SHOWDOWN

As Susan was beamed up towards Gallaxhar's spaceship, Insectosaurus shot a thread of silk at her, pulling her back towards Earth. "Way to go, Insecto!" cheered The Missing Link.
Then Gallaxhar fired at Insectosaurus, hitting him and knocking him out. Susan saw him fall. "Insectosaurus! No!" she cried as the beam pulled her relentlessly into the alien ship. The Missing Link, rushed to Insectosaurus's aid. "It's going to be all right. Look at me! Don't you close those eyes. Don't you dare close those eyes!" But his giant eyelids gradually slid shut.

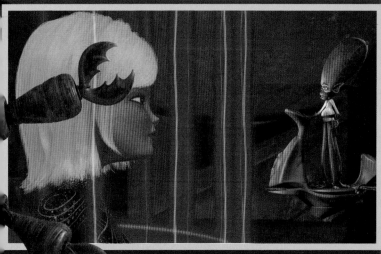

Inside the mothership, Susan found herself dressed in a space suit in a room full of alien robots just like the one she had fought in San Francisco. Gallaxhar appeared out of the shadows, flying on a hoverboard and imprisoned her in a narrow energy field.

"Muah-ha-ha-hah. You must be terrified. You wake up in a strange place, wearing strange clothes, imprisoned by a strange being floating on a strange hovering device. Strange, isn't it?" he said.

"Hardly. It's not the first time," replied Susan.

"Wow, you really get around." Then, remembering his purpose for capturing Susan he declared: "To the extraction chamber!"

The energy field carried Susan into the main area of the mothership.

"Look, what is it that you want from me?" demanded Susan.

"You have stolen what is rightfully mine," said Gallaxhar.

"I didn't steal anything from you!" she replied.

"Your enormous, grotesque body contains Quantonium, the most powerful substance in the Universe. Did you really think you could keep it from me?" asked Gallaxhar.

"That's what all this is about? You destroyed San Francisco, you, you terrified millions of people… you killed my friend. Just to get to me?!" exclaimed Susan.

"A-ca-ca-ca! Silence! Your voice is grating on my ear nubs. It's a shame you won't be around to see what the power of Quantonium can do in the tentacles of someone who knows how to use it," said the overlord.

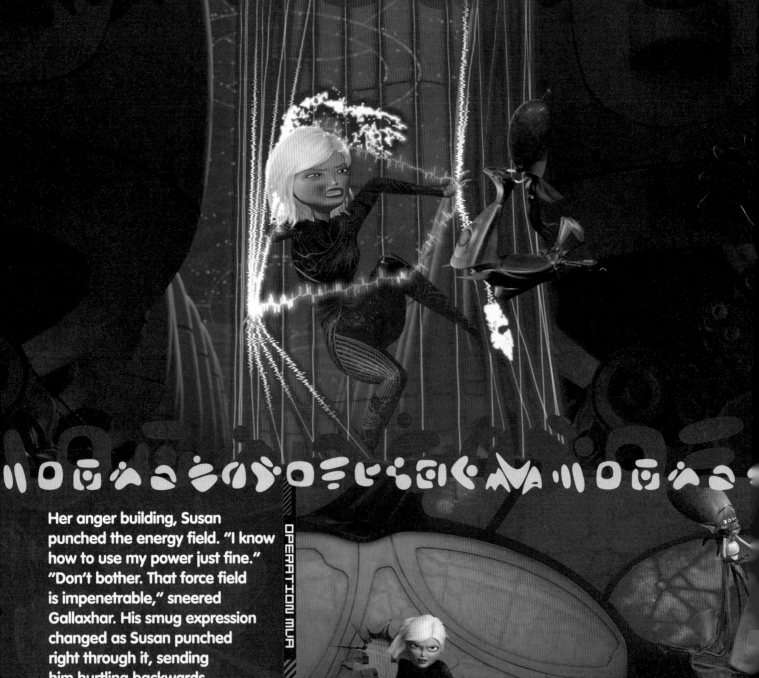

Her anger building, Susan punched the energy field. "I know how to use my power just fine." "Don't bother. That force field is impenetrable," sneered Gallaxhar. His smug expression changed as Susan punched right through it, sending him hurtling backwards. "What the Flagnard?" he exclaimed. Susan raced towards Gallaxhar, who zoomed away on his hoverboard. Using a control panel on his board, Gallaxhar shut the bay door behind him as he passed through it, separating himself from Susan. "Ha! That should stop your puny…" he laughed. Without stopping Susan smashed into the door, demolishing it, and continued her pursuit. "Computer, close door hangar two!" ordered Gallaxhar. "Close door hangar three! Door hangar four! Oh, close them all!" But each time a door closed in front of her, Susan smashed her way straight through it,

gaining on Gallaxhar. As they reached the ship's bridge, Susan swiped the alien overlord and knocked him off his hoverboard, and when he picked himself up the two stood face to face. Gallaxhar ran to the controls, pulled a lever, and the extraction chamber descended around Susan. "Computer, begin extraction!" ordered Gallaxhar. Even as Susan was growing smaller and the extraction process took effect, she put up a fight.

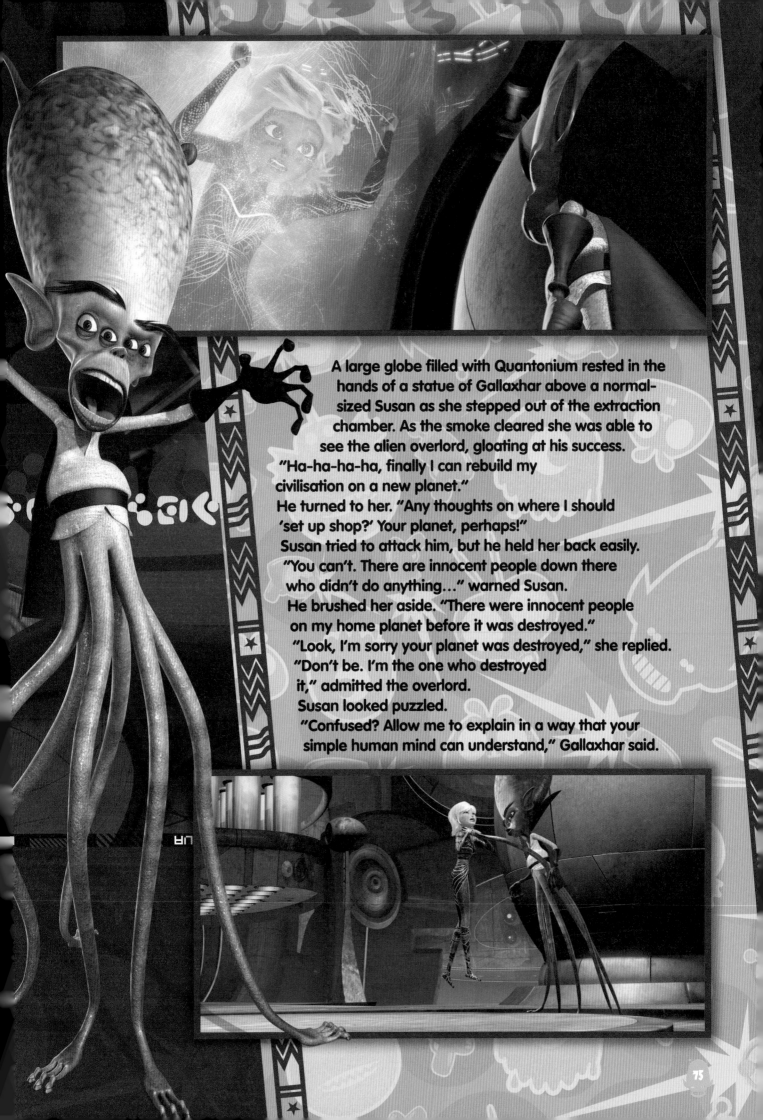

A large globe filled with Quantonium rested in the hands of a statue of Gallaxhar above a normal-sized Susan as she stepped out of the extraction chamber. As the smoke cleared she was able to see the alien overlord, gloating at his success.

"Ha-ha-ha-ha, finally I can rebuild my civilisation on a new planet."

He turned to her. "Any thoughts on where I should 'set up shop?' Your planet, perhaps!"

Susan tried to attack him, but he held her back easily.

"You can't. There are innocent people down there who didn't do anything…" warned Susan.

He brushed her aside. "There were innocent people on my home planet before it was destroyed."

"Look, I'm sorry your planet was destroyed," she replied.

"Don't be. I'm the one who destroyed it," admitted the overlord.

Susan looked puzzled.

"Confused? Allow me to explain in a way that your simple human mind can understand," Gallaxhar said.

Gallaxhar stepped inside a metal cloning pod with a lid that stamped down and lifted back up, making thousands of exact copies of him each time. "Many Zentons ago, when I was but a squidling, I found out that my parents…" he began, as the lid stamped down and then lifted back up, briefly drowning his words, and creating a group of Gallaxhar clones. "… no child should ever have to endure that! So I went on the road with a giant…" he continued. Once again the machine's lid stamped down to create more clones. "… and soon thereafter was married. Things were going well until she wanted to…" Once more he disappeared and his story was interrupted. "But I have told you too much already…" Gallaxhar stepped out of the machine. "Let the birth of my new planet, Gallaxhar's Wet and Wild, begin!" he roared. Suddenly, rows of hundreds of thousands of Gallaxhars were being created by giant machines. The clones marched forward like an army.

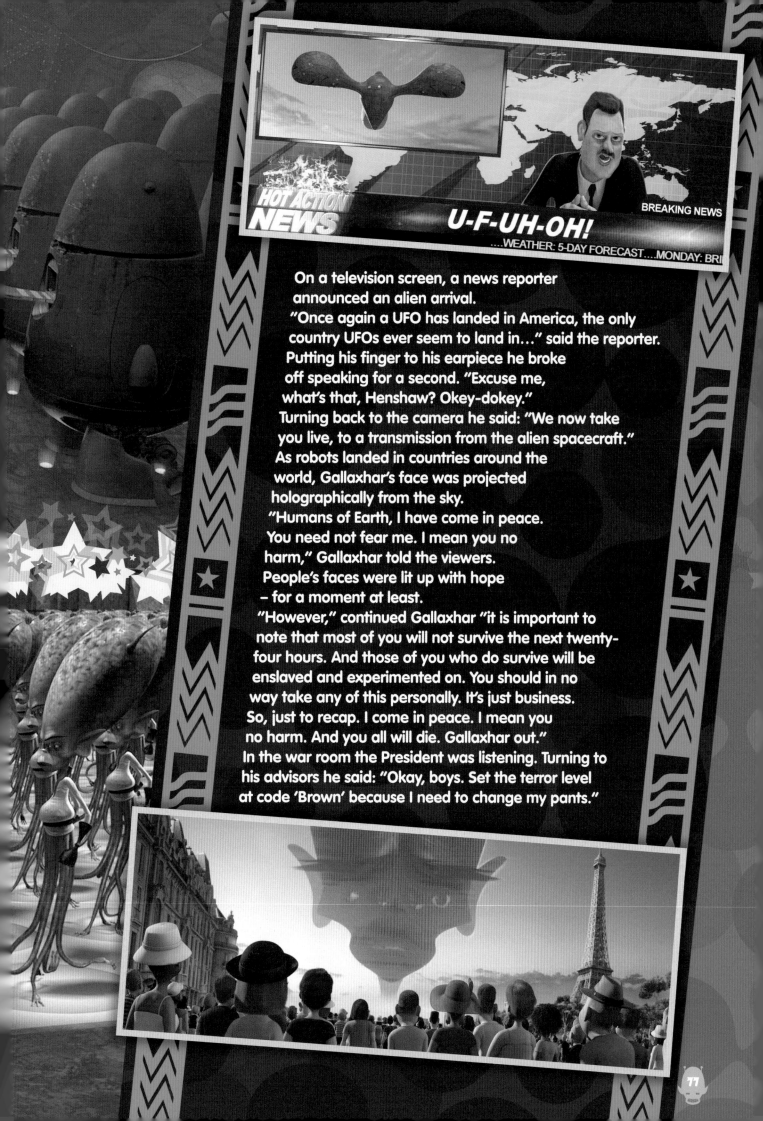

BREAKING NEWS

U-F-UH-OH!

....WEATHER: 5-DAY FORECAST....MONDAY: BRI

On a television screen, a news reporter announced an alien arrival.

"Once again a UFO has landed in America, the only country UFOs ever seem to land in…" said the reporter. Putting his finger to his earpiece he broke off speaking for a second. "Excuse me, what's that, Henshaw? Okey-dokey."

Turning back to the camera he said: "We now take you live, to a transmission from the alien spacecraft."

As robots landed in countries around the world, Gallaxhar's face was projected holographically from the sky.

"Humans of Earth, I have come in peace. You need not fear me. I mean you no harm," Gallaxhar told the viewers.

People's faces were lit up with hope – for a moment at least.

"However," continued Gallaxhar "it is important to note that most of you will not survive the next twenty-four hours. And those of you who do survive will be enslaved and experimented on. You should in no way take any of this personally. It's just business. So, just to recap. I come in peace. I mean you no harm. And you all will die. Gallaxhar out."

In the war room the President was listening. Turning to his advisors he said: "Okay, boys. Set the terror level at code 'Brown' because I need to change my pants."

77

The Missing Link stood alongside the body
of Insectosaurus, which was now covered in
a silky substance. B.O.B. and Dr. Cockroach
stood nearby, shaking their heads.
"What are we going to do now,
Doc?" asked B.O.B.
"I… I don't know," admitted Dr. Cockroach.
"You are flipping me out here, because
you always know," argued B.O.B.
"And if you don't know, well that
means no one knows. And if you think
about that then who knows? Who
knows if we're even here? If we exist?
And if you think about that and what
you don't know combined with what
I do know and what we both don't…"
Dr. Cockroach slapped B.O.B.
to stop him rambling.
"Thank you, Doc," said B.O.B.
The Missing Link intervened. "Here's what
I know. I'll tell you what we're gonna do.
We're not gonna let Insecto die in vain.
We're gonna get up there, find Susan, and
we're going to take that alien down. And
I know just the guy who can help us."

Inside the transporter plane, the monsters had been equipped with jet packs to reach the alien spaceship. General Monger paced up and down explaining the plan.

"All right, gentlemen. You got enough juice in those jet packs to get you up there. But not enough to make it home. I'll come get you if I can. If I don't, it means I'm dead. Or late," stated Monger. Softening his tone Monger added: "I've been your warden for close to fifty years. That is no longer the case." He lifted his hand in a military salute. "And for what it's worth…"

"That's rude!" said B.O.B. "What did we do?"

"No, B.O.B. That's not rude, that's a sign of respect," pointed out Dr. Cockroach. The transporter plane's door opened and the monsters fired up their jet packs and set off for the alien spaceship on their mission to rescue Susan.

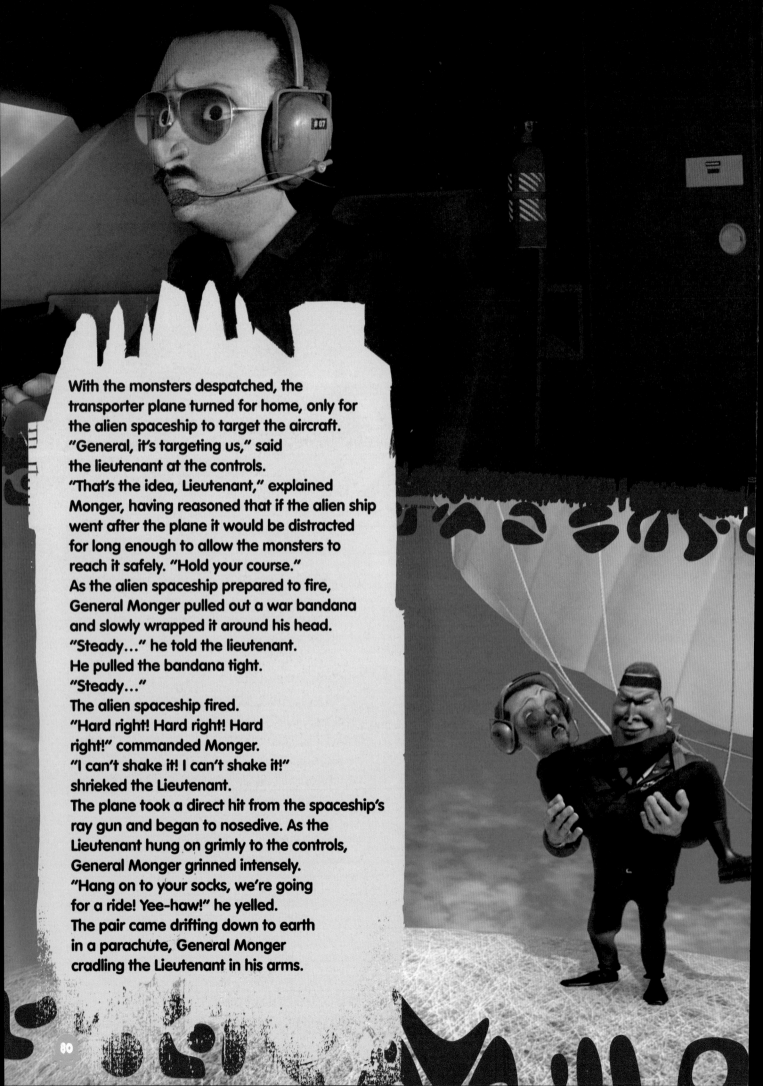

With the monsters despatched, the transporter plane turned for home, only for the alien spaceship to target the aircraft. "General, it's targeting us," said the lieutenant at the controls.

"That's the idea, Lieutenant," explained Monger, having reasoned that if the alien ship went after the plane it would be distracted for long enough to allow the monsters to reach it safely. "Hold your course."

As the alien spaceship prepared to fire, General Monger pulled out a war bandana and slowly wrapped it around his head. "Steady…" he told the lieutenant.

He pulled the bandana tight.

"Steady…"

The alien spaceship fired.

"Hard right! Hard right! Hard right!" commanded Monger.

"I can't shake it! I can't shake it!" shrieked the Lieutenant.

The plane took a direct hit from the spaceship's ray gun and began to nosedive. As the Lieutenant hung on grimly to the controls, General Monger grinned intensely.

"Hang on to your socks, we're going for a ride! Yee-haw!" he yelled.

The pair came drifting down to earth in a parachute, General Monger cradling the Lieutenant in his arms.

Inside the spaceship, the monsters peered
nervously round from behind an inactive robot.
"Ka-ka-ka-kaw! Ka kaw!" called B.O.B.
"Shh-shh!" reprimanded Dr. Cockroach. "Who
are you signalling? We're right here."
The Missing Link silenced them as several
rows of giant robot invaders came past.
Meanwhile, Gallaxhar was marshalling his
newly cloned troops, addressing a large
number assembled in front of him.
"Clone…"
"Hail Gallaxhar," they chorused together.
"No, you. Not that one. Yes, you! Take the prisoner to the
incinerator. She's useless to us now," said the alien overlord.
"Hail Gallaxhar!" said the clone, moving towards Susan.
"Hail me," said Gallaxhar.
The clone led Susan away as the monsters watched
from the tunnel above the causeway.
"Wow. Ginormica ain't so… ginormic any
more," observed The Missing Link.
"How are we supposed to get to her?" asked
Dr. Cockroach. "There's too many of them.
It's impossible," said The Missing Link.
B.O.B. suddenly piped up: "I may not have
a brain, gentlemen, but I have an idea."

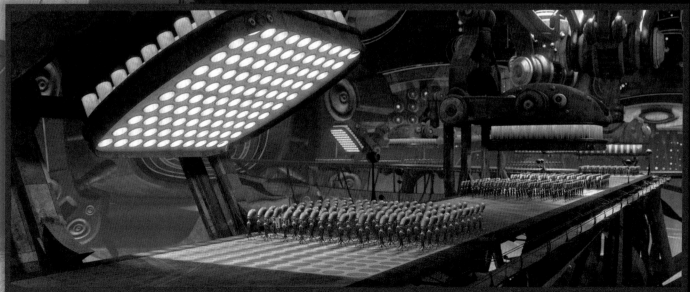

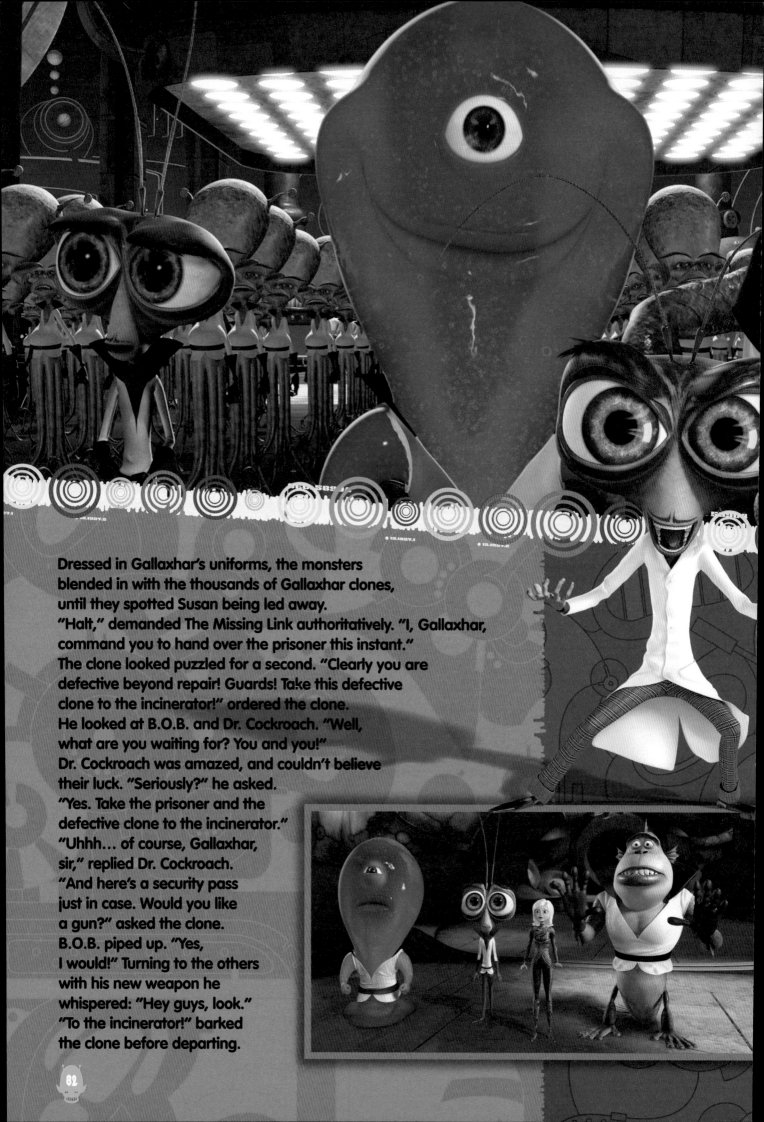

Dressed in Gallaxhar's uniforms, the monsters
blended in with the thousands of Gallaxhar clones,
until they spotted Susan being led away.

"Halt," demanded The Missing Link authoritatively. "I, Gallaxhar,
command you to hand over the prisoner this instant."
The clone looked puzzled for a second. "Clearly you are
defective beyond repair! Guards! Take this defective
clone to the incinerator!" ordered the clone.
He looked at B.O.B. and Dr. Cockroach. "Well,
what are you waiting for? You and you!"
Dr. Cockroach was amazed, and couldn't believe
their luck. "Seriously?" he asked.
"Yes. Take the prisoner and the
defective clone to the incinerator."
"Uhhh… of course, Gallaxhar,
sir," replied Dr. Cockroach.
"And here's a security pass
just in case. Would you like
a gun?" asked the clone.
B.O.B. piped up. "Yes,
I would!" Turning to the others
with his new weapon he
whispered: "Hey guys, look."
"To the incinerator!" barked
the clone before departing.

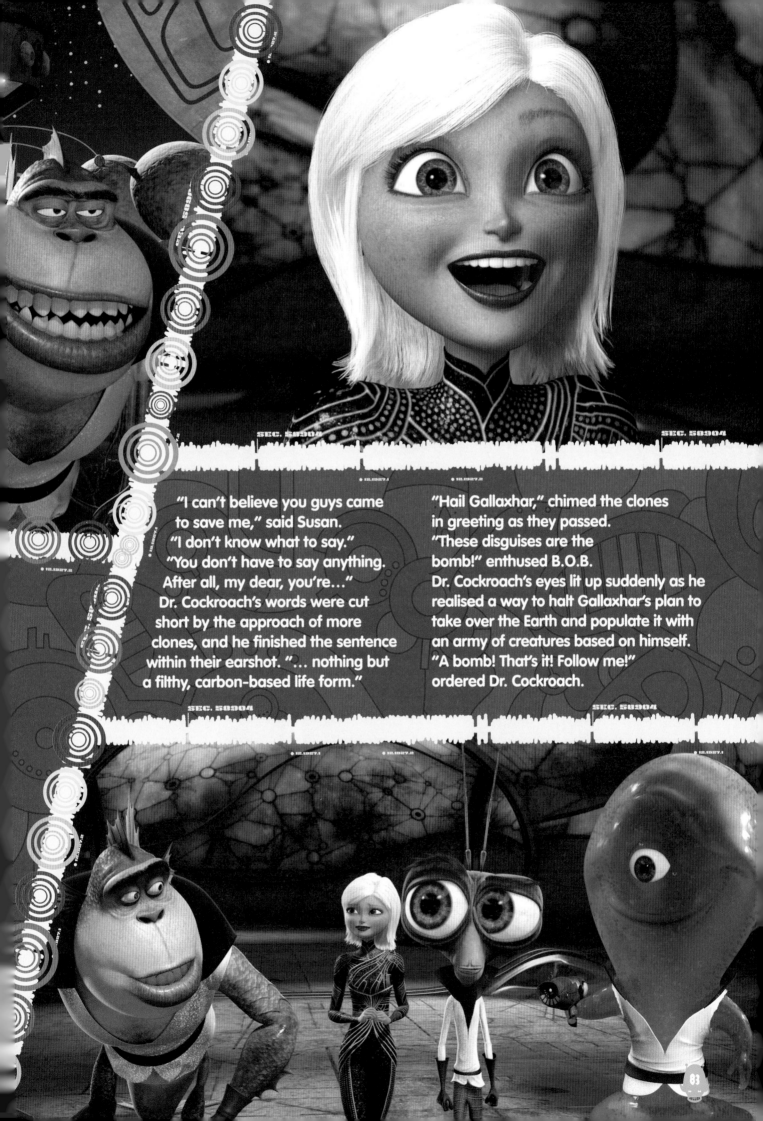

SEC. 58904   SEC. 58904

"I can't believe you guys came to save me," said Susan. "I don't know what to say." "You don't have to say anything. After all, my dear, you're…" Dr. Cockroach's words were cut short by the approach of more clones, and he finished the sentence within their earshot. "… nothing but a filthy, carbon-based life form."

"Hail Gallaxhar," chimed the clones in greeting as they passed. "These disguises are the bomb!" enthused B.O.B. Dr. Cockroach's eyes lit up suddenly as he realised a way to halt Gallaxhar's plan to take over the Earth and populate it with an army of creatures based on himself. "A bomb! That's it! Follow me!" ordered Dr. Cockroach.

SEC. 58904   SEC. 58904

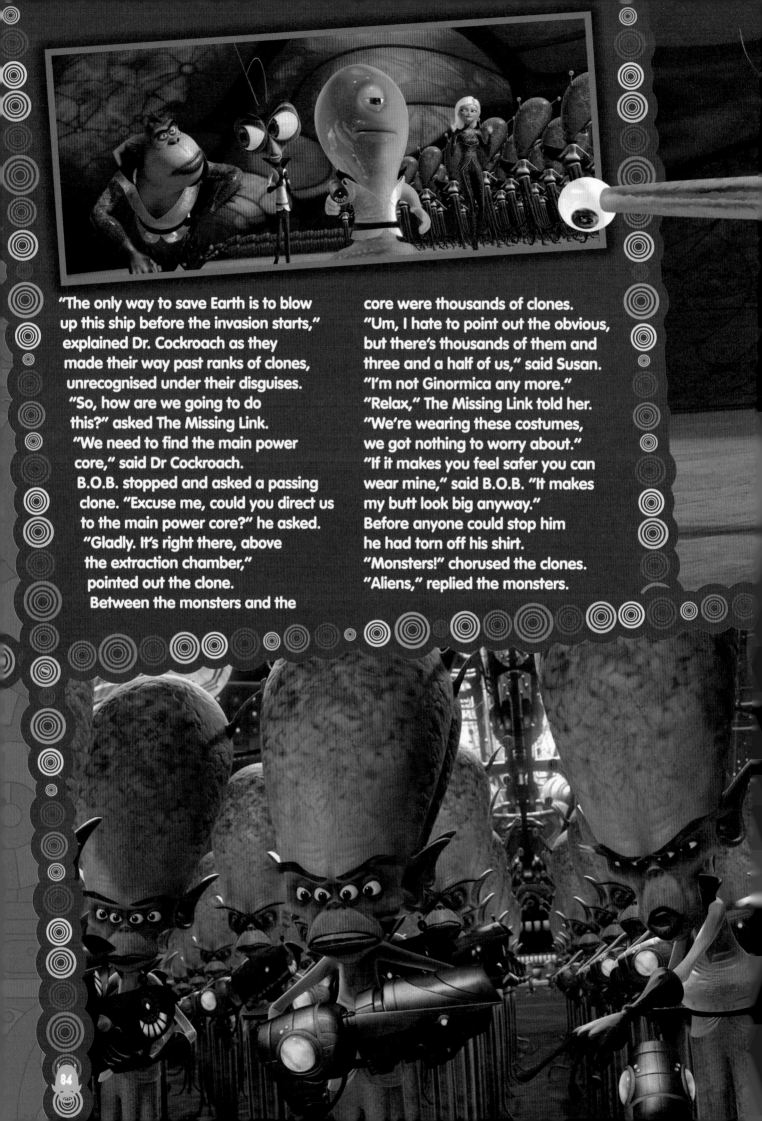

"The only way to save Earth is to blow up this ship before the invasion starts," explained Dr. Cockroach as they made their way past ranks of clones, unrecognised under their disguises.

"So, how are we going to do this?" asked The Missing Link.

"We need to find the main power core," said Dr Cockroach.

B.O.B. stopped and asked a passing clone. "Excuse me, could you direct us to the main power core?" he asked.

"Gladly. It's right there, above the extraction chamber," pointed out the clone.

Between the monsters and the core were thousands of clones.

"Um, I hate to point out the obvious, but there's thousands of them and three and a half of us," said Susan. "I'm not Ginormica any more."

"Relax," The Missing Link told her. "We're wearing these costumes, we got nothing to worry about."

"If it makes you feel safer you can wear mine," said B.O.B. "It makes my butt look big anyway."

Before anyone could stop him he had torn off his shirt.

"Monsters!" chorused the clones.

"Aliens," replied the monsters.

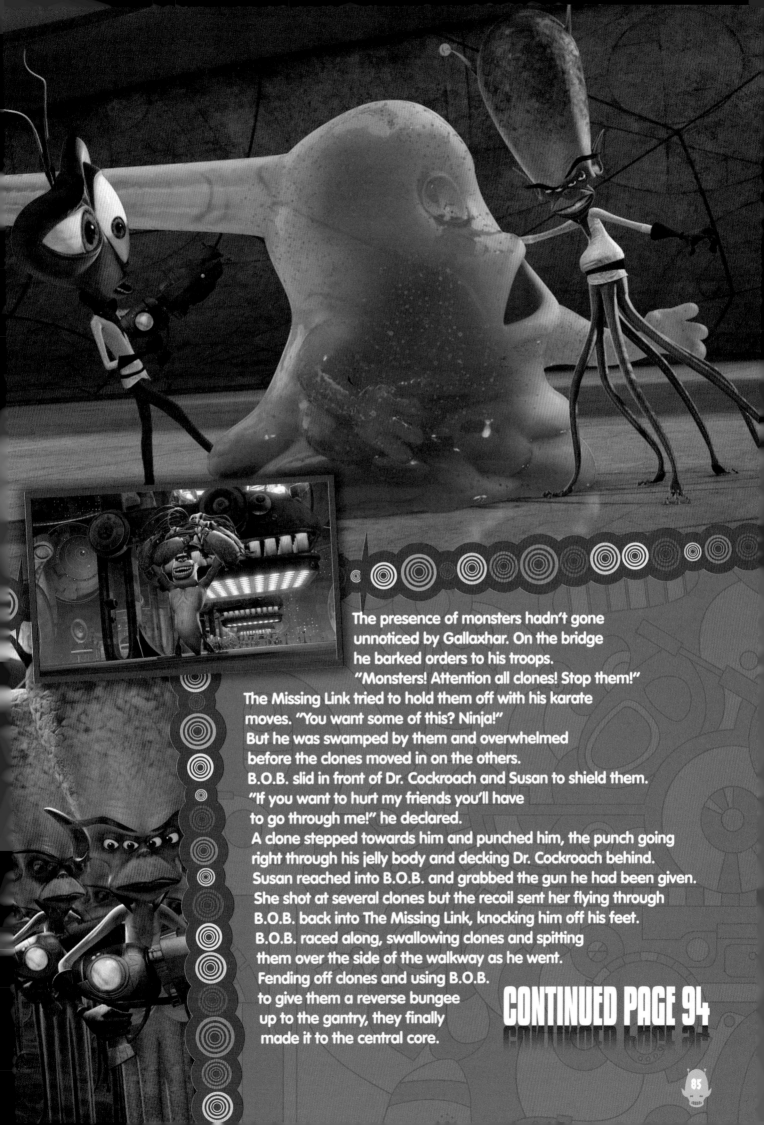

The presence of monsters hadn't gone
unnoticed by Gallaxhar. On the bridge
he barked orders to his troops.
"Monsters! Attention all clones! Stop them!"
The Missing Link tried to hold them off with his karate
moves. "You want some of this? Ninja!"
But he was swamped by them and overwhelmed
before the clones moved in on the others.
B.O.B. slid in front of Dr. Cockroach and Susan to shield them.
"If you want to hurt my friends you'll have
to go through me!" he declared.
A clone stepped towards him and punched him, the punch going
right through his jelly body and decking Dr. Cockroach behind.
Susan reached into B.O.B. and grabbed the gun he had been given.
She shot at several clones but the recoil sent her flying through
B.O.B. back into The Missing Link, knocking him off his feet.
B.O.B. raced along, swallowing clones and spitting
them over the side of the walkway as he went.
Fending off clones and using B.O.B.
to give them a reverse bungee
up to the gantry, they finally
made it to the central core.

CONTINUED PAGE 94

ARE YOU A MONSTER OR AN ALIEN

START HERE

AN ALIEN CALLS ROUND FOR TEA. WHAT DO YOU DO?

Invite him in and get out the best cups and flying saucers

Tell him you're too busy doing your homework?

Look past them to see if there's still time to call the Alien back?

He accidentally slops some tea on the tablecloth. Do you...?

Invite him in but say you're clean out of digestives?

One starts to blow on his hands and stamp his feet. Do you...?

Say it needed washing anyway?

Fetch a cloth and start sponging frantically?

The Alien wants to have a go on your new bike. Do you...?

Agree with them that the weather is chilly?

The Alien lets out a loud belch. Do you...?

Say: "Pardon me" and look embarrassed?

Say yes but secretly hope his feet won't reach the pedals?

Pretend it's got a puncture?

Do the same to make him feel at home?

Do nothing and hope no one noticed?

Carry it outside for him to try?

ABSOLUTELY ALIEN

ALMOST EXCLUSIVELY ALIEN

MOSTLY ALIEN

ALIENISH

BORDERLINE ALIEN

86

People generally come in two types — cat or dog lovers, cricket or football fans, and monsters or aliens.

The question is, which are you?
Answer the questions below to find out.

ENCLOSURE

No sooner has he gone than a group of Monsters turns up. Do you...?

Tell them how glad you are to see them?

The jelly-like one sits too close to the radiator and starts to melt. Do you...?

Reluctantly let them in but keep an eye on them in case they turn ugly?

Invite them in but ask them to wipe all their feet?

Hand round spoons and tell everyone to help themselves?

Fetch a bag of frozen peas for him to sit on?

They have never seen a sofa before and start using it as a trampoline. Do you...?

Put some loud music on to encourage them?

Just try to avoid slipping in the ooze creeping across the floor?

Ask them where they've parked their spaceship?

Tell them if they slip down the back they'll never get out alive?

Hope one of them breaks a leg and brings things to a halt?

ALMOST ALIEN

BORDERLINE MONSTROUS

MIDDLINGLY MONSTROUS

MOSTLY MONSTROUS

INCURABLY MONSTROUS

INSIPID INSECTO

Give Insectosaurus a bit of a buzz by colouring him in.

● 12.1927.1   ● 12.1927.2

B.O.B.
A-JOB

We've been having a bit of fun with B.O.B. and tweaking these pictures a bit by changing a few details. Wobble up close to the page and see if you can spot all five of them.

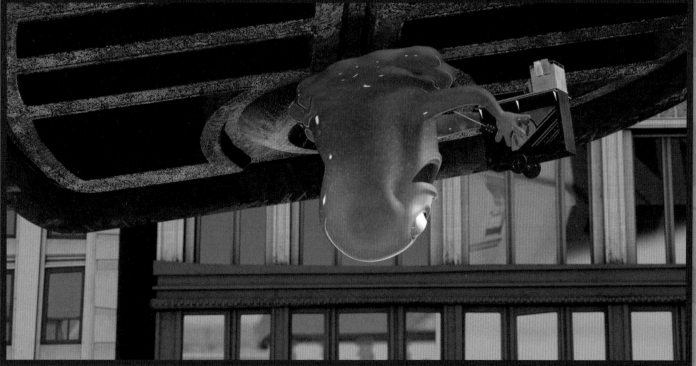

SEC. 58904

● 12.1927.1   ● 12.1927.2

FIND THE FEATURES

Take a close look at this scene and see if you can spot the details shown at the bottom of the page. Tick them off as you find them.

FISHY FRIENDS

Fit the names of some of The Missing Link's freshwater fishy friends into the correct spaces on the puzzle to put a smile on his face.

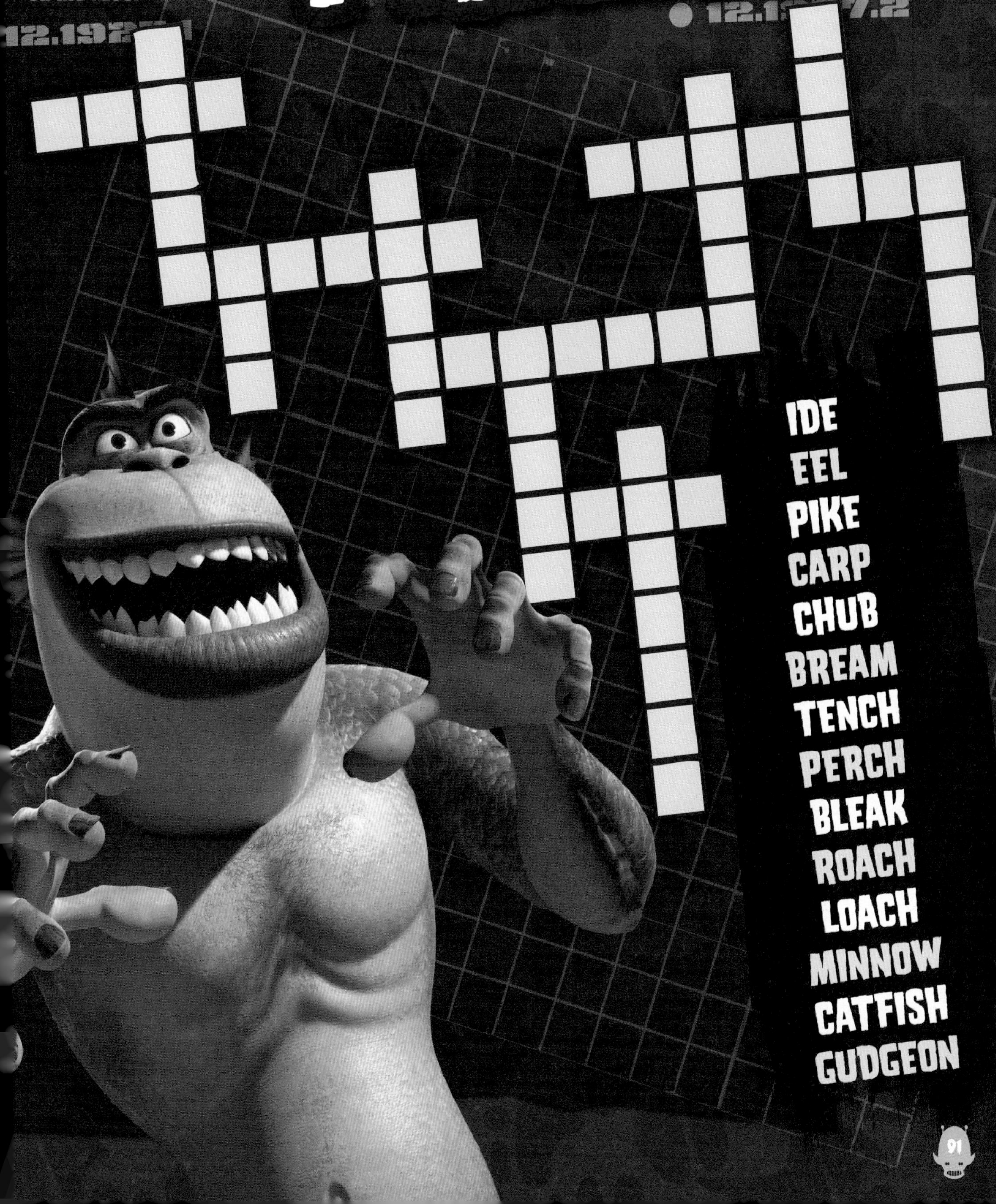

IDE
EEL
PIKE
CARP
CHUB
BREAM
TENCH
PERCH
BLEAK
ROACH
LOACH
MINNOW
CATFISH
GUDGEON

91

QUIZ

Use your knowledge of the story to solve the following multiple-choice questions.

1. What codename did the technicians use to alert the Government to the arrival of the meteor?

a) Mayday
b) Nemoy
c) OMG

ANSWER

2. What item belonging to Susan flew off and flattened a fleeing guest when she grew to 50 ft tall?

a) Her hairband
b) Her shoe
c) Her garter

ANSWER

3. What did the multi-tentacled Gallaxhar describe himself as, back in his younger days?

a) A squidling
b) A quizling
c) A widdling

ANSWER

4. How long had General Monger been a warden to the monsters?

a) thirty years
b) fifty years
c) a hundred years

ANSWER

5. What shape did Derek make with his hands when telling TV viewers it was his wedding day?

a) a high five
b) a fist
c) a heart

ANSWER

6. What was B.O.B. chatting up at the party at Susan's parents?

a) a jelly
b) an ice-cream
c) a strawberry blancmange

ANSWER

93

CORE WAR

The central core of the mothership was its nerve centre, and the computer was like a giant brain ensuring its smooth operation. Dr. Cockroach knew that if he could programme the computer to self-destruct he could destroy the alien spaceship.

"O.M.G.," gasped Dr. Cockroach, realising that even his impressive brainpower would be taxed by Gallaxhar's creation.

The computer sensed the monster's presence. "Warning. Intruder," it declared.

Dr. Cockroach stepped on to the colourful control tower floor, which beeped as he did so. "You'll never figure out my colour code," boasted the computer.

Dr. Cockroach looked down at the coloured panels beneath his feet. "Of course! This computer operates on a hexadecimal colour code system. If I can hack it, I can set this ship to self-destruct. This won't be but a moment," he declared confidently.

He started to dance, tapping different coloured panels in a complicated sequence, getting faster and faster as he went. "Red, green, blue, yellow, orange, baby blue, purple, pink, mauve, gold, brown ochre, avocado, Adobe glow, hey!" called out Dr. Cockroach.

Susan looked out of the portal to see clones swarming up towards them. "Hurry up! Hurry!" she urged.

Unconcerned, B.O.B. was enjoying watching Dr. Cockroach so much he began to clap along, prompting the mad scientist to start hitting dance-floor poses while continuing to tap out the sequence with his feet.

"So. You think you can dance Doctor?" sneered the computer.

"Oh, you ain't seen nothing yet!" he boasted. "Quickstep... jazz... rumba..."

By now the clones were climbing up to the portal and closing in on them fast. Susan slammed the door closed, trapping some of their slimy tentacles.

The Missing Link was also getting worried. "Doc, c'mon, let's hurry."

"Your busted, tired dance moves are no match for my security protocols," sneered the computer. Spurred on by its mocking tone, Dr. Cockroach danced even faster, cranking out moves from decades of dance, his feet a blur.

"There's one thing you don't know about me, my dear," he told Susan. "My Ph.D. is in dance!"

Suddenly the core started to malfunction, its computer code cracked. Dr. Cockroach's superior brainpower and knowledge of dance moves had beaten it and brought about meltdown.

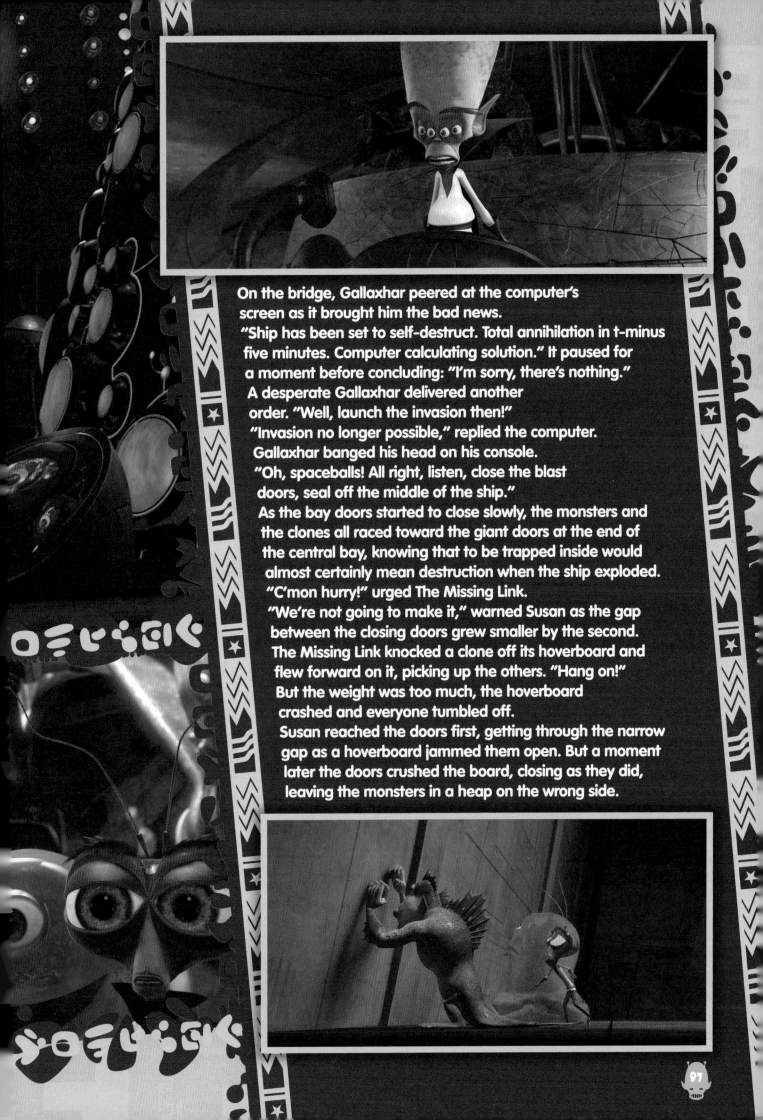

On the bridge, Gallaxhar peered at the computer's screen as it brought him the bad news.

"Ship has been set to self-destruct. Total annihilation in t-minus five minutes. Computer calculating solution." It paused for a moment before concluding: "I'm sorry, there's nothing."

A desperate Gallaxhar delivered another order. "Well, launch the invasion then!"

"Invasion no longer possible," replied the computer. Gallaxhar banged his head on his console.

"Oh, spaceballs! All right, listen, close the blast doors, seal off the middle of the ship."

As the bay doors started to close slowly, the monsters and the clones all raced toward the giant doors at the end of the central bay, knowing that to be trapped inside would almost certainly mean destruction when the ship exploded.

"C'mon hurry!" urged The Missing Link.

"We're not going to make it," warned Susan as the gap between the closing doors grew smaller by the second. The Missing Link knocked a clone off its hoverboard and flew forward on it, picking up the others. "Hang on!" But the weight was too much, the hoverboard crashed and everyone tumbled off.

Susan reached the doors first, getting through the narrow gap as a hoverboard jammed them open. But a moment later the doors crushed the board, closing as they did, leaving the monsters in a heap on the wrong side.

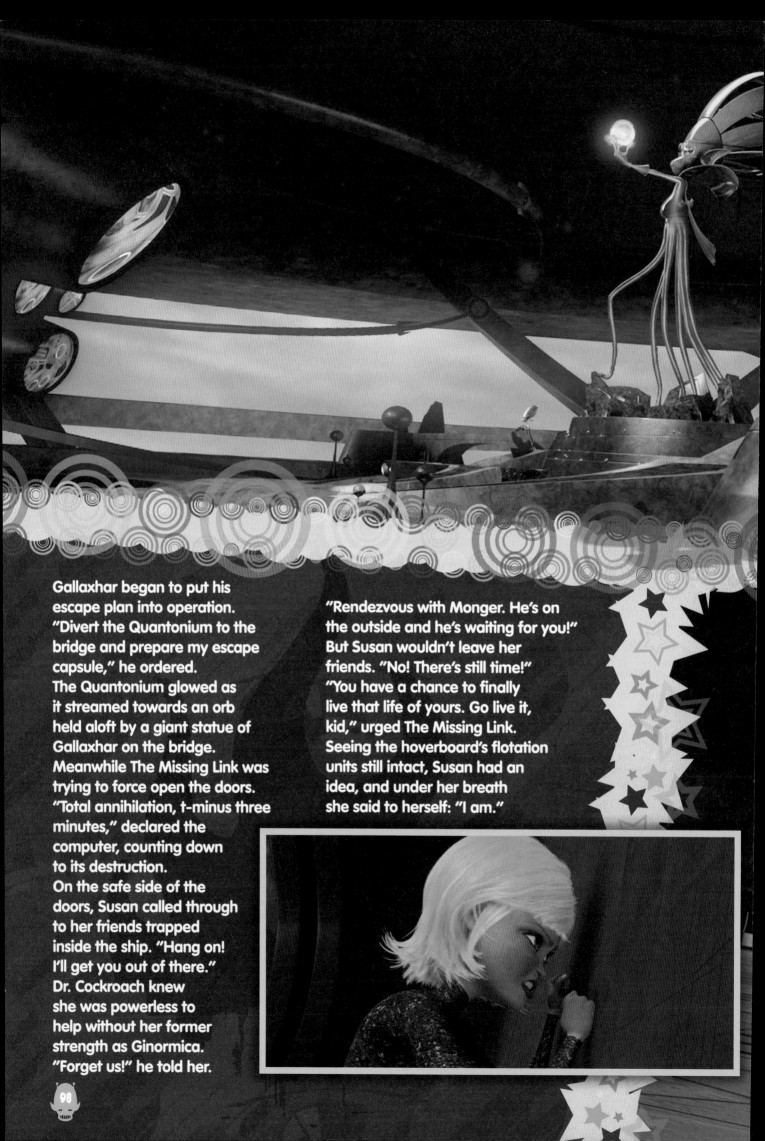

Gallaxhar began to put his escape plan into operation. "Divert the Quantonium to the bridge and prepare my escape capsule," he ordered.
The Quantonium glowed as it streamed towards an orb held aloft by a giant statue of Gallaxhar on the bridge.
Meanwhile The Missing Link was trying to force open the doors. "Total annihilation, t-minus three minutes," declared the computer, counting down to its destruction.
On the safe side of the doors, Susan called through to her friends trapped inside the ship. "Hang on! I'll get you out of there." Dr. Cockroach knew she was powerless to help without her former strength as Ginormica. "Forget us!" he told her.

"Rendezvous with Monger. He's on the outside and he's waiting for you!" But Susan wouldn't leave her friends. "No! There's still time!" "You have a chance to finally live that life of yours. Go live it, kid," urged The Missing Link. Seeing the hoverboard's flotation units still intact, Susan had an idea, and under her breath she said to herself: "I am."

Susan flew through the ship watched by a hologram of Gallaxhar's head. "Female carbon-based life form not contained," warned the computer. "Oh, she's good." "No, she's a real pain in the zaxon!" complained Gallaxhar. "Attention robot probes. Crush the Earthling!" As Susan raced into the hangar the giant robot army came to life, attempting to capture her. She flew around them, confusing them and causing the lumbering robots to crash into each other.

The computer issued another update. "Robot bay
has been destroyed. Invasion no longer possible."
"Fire phaziod cannon!" barked Gallaxhar.
As the cannon shot zoomed towards Susan, she
dodged the phaziod beam and headed to do
battle with Gallaxhar on the ship's bridge.
Flinging a piece of the hoverboard, she knocked the
gun that Gallaxhar had just lifted out of his hand.
As Gallaxhar was blown backwards,
the gun slid across the floor.
Susan entered the bridge. "I'm warning
you, Gallaxhar. Let my friends go."
The computer issued another update. "Quantonium
has been successfully diverted to the bridge."
Just then the head of the giant Gallaxhar
statue opened to reveal an escape pod.
"Escape pod ready for transport," announced the computer.
Gallaxhar had lost none of his superior tone. "You couldn't
defeat me when you had the Quantonium, you're not
going to do it now. Have fun exploding!" he taunted.
With that, Gallaxhar ran for the escape pod and
started to climb on board. However, Susan yanked
him down and the pair crashed to the floor.

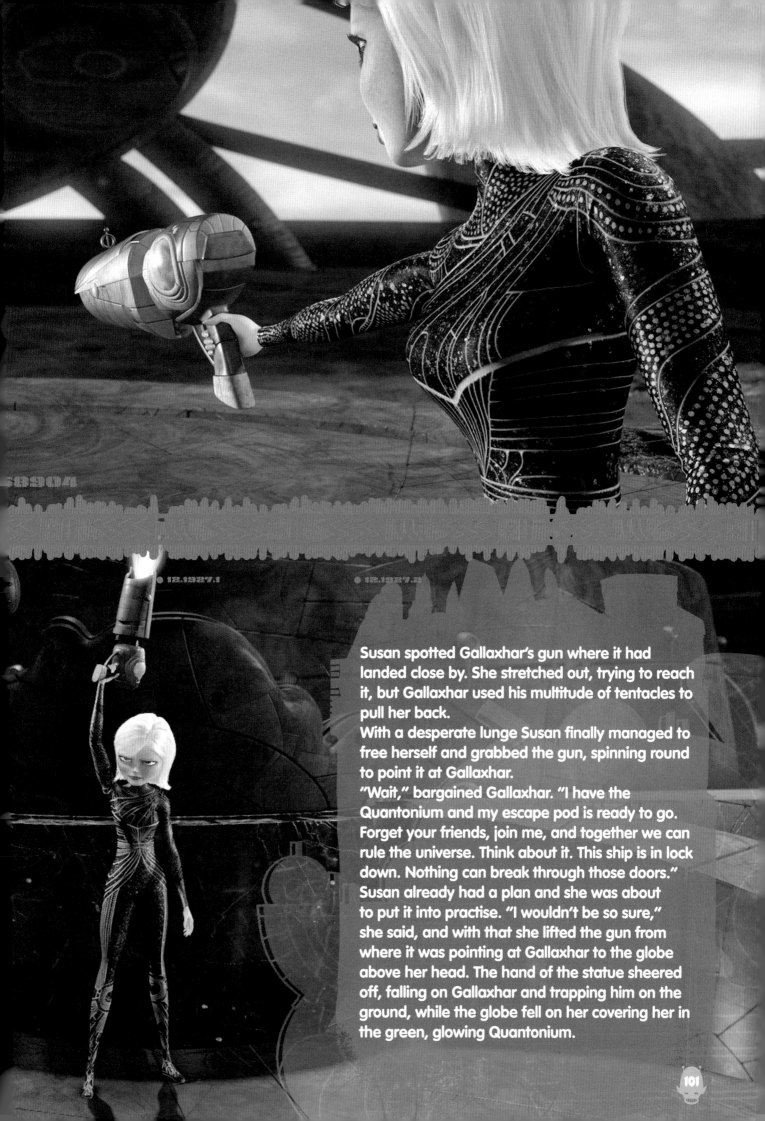

Susan spotted Gallaxhar's gun where it had landed close by. She stretched out, trying to reach it, but Gallaxhar used his multitude of tentacles to pull her back.

With a desperate lunge Susan finally managed to free herself and grabbed the gun, spinning round to point it at Gallaxhar.

"Wait," bargained Gallaxhar. "I have the Quantonium and my escape pod is ready to go. Forget your friends, join me, and together we can rule the universe. Think about it. This ship is in lock down. Nothing can break through those doors."

Susan already had a plan and she was about to put it into practise. "I wouldn't be so sure," she said, and with that she lifted the gun from where it was pointing at Gallaxhar to the globe above her head. The hand of the statue sheered off, falling on Gallaxhar and trapping him on the ground, while the globe fell on her covering her in the green, glowing Quantonium.

SEC. 58904

Back in the ship's inner chamber, the monsters listened
dejectedly as the computer counted down to destruction
and debris crashed down around them.

"Total annihilation, t-minus one minute," it informed them.

"It's been an honour knowing you Doc," The
Missing Link told Dr. Cockroach.

"The feeling's mutual, my friend," replied the Doctor.
Only B.O.B., with his absence of a brain, remained upbeat.

"I'll see you guys tomorrow for lunch," he told them.

Dr. Cockroach and The Missing Link looked at each other
and decided to play along to avoid upsetting him.

"That's right, B.O.B." said The Missing Link.

"And there will be candy and cake and balloons," added Dr. Cockroach.

"Cake and balloons for lunch?" said an excited B.O.B.

"It's going to be the best day ever! I love you guys!"
Just then a huge chunk of machinery plunged towards them
and was about to crush them when Susan caught it.

"Hogan's Goat! It's Susan!" said an astonished Dr. Cockroach.

"Correction Doc, it's Ginormica," added The Missing Link.

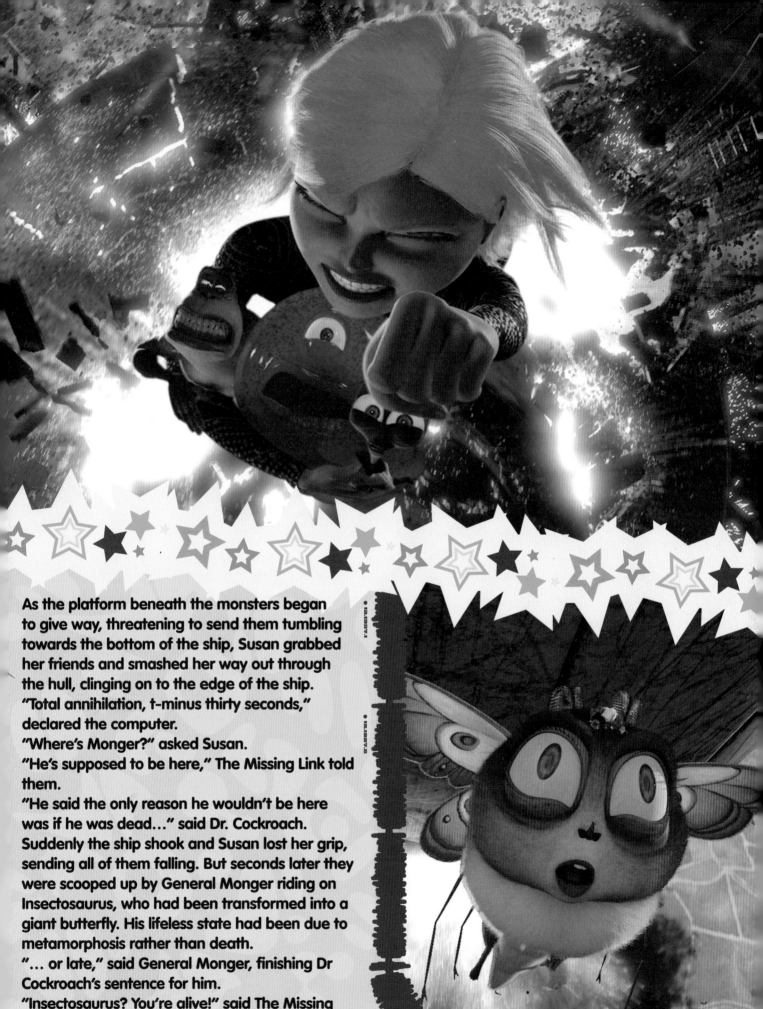

As the platform beneath the monsters began to give way, threatening to send them tumbling towards the bottom of the ship, Susan grabbed her friends and smashed her way out through the hull, clinging on to the edge of the ship.

"Total annihilation, t-minus thirty seconds," declared the computer.

"Where's Monger?" asked Susan.

"He's supposed to be here," The Missing Link told them.

"He said the only reason he wouldn't be here was if he was dead…" said Dr. Cockroach. Suddenly the ship shook and Susan lost her grip, sending all of them falling. But seconds later they were scooped up by General Monger riding on Insectosaurus, who had been transformed into a giant butterfly. His lifeless state had been due to metamorphosis rather than death.

"… or late," said General Monger, finishing Dr Cockroach's sentence for him.

"Insectosaurus? You're alive!" said The Missing Link as the butterfly flew them to safety away from the doomed ship.

Back on board what was
left of the alien spaceship,
Gallaxhar climbed into his
escape pod. However, his efforts
to start the engine produced only a
coughing sound from under the bonnet.
"C'mon, c'mon!" urged a frustrated
and desperate Gallaxhar.
The computer neared the end of its
countdown. "Five…. four… three…"
Gallaxhar tried again, but this time a red petrol
pump symbol lit up on the dashboard.
"What idiot forgot to refuel the escape
capsule?" asked Gallaxhar.
"You did Gallaxhar," the computer informed him. "Two…"
"Fair enough," said Gallaxhar, now resigned to his fate.
"One," said the computer.
Silence.
"Hmm. Nothing happened. Maybe my
count was…" said the computer.
BOOM! The mothership exploded in an
orange fireball.

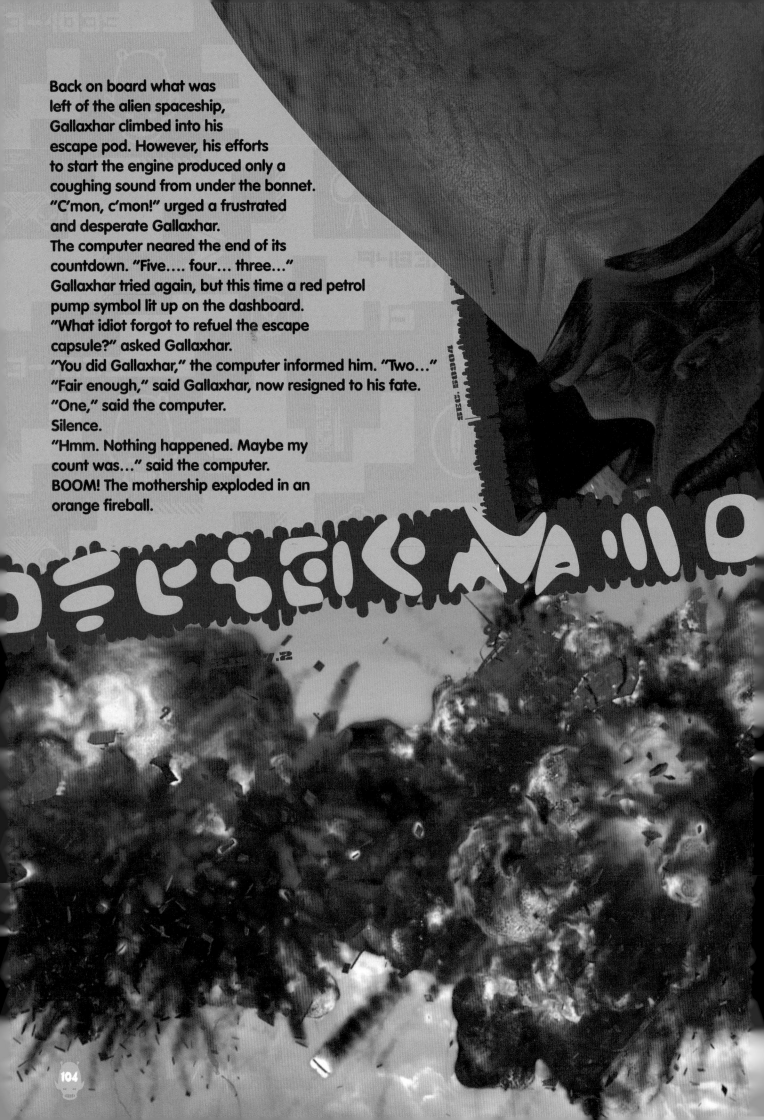

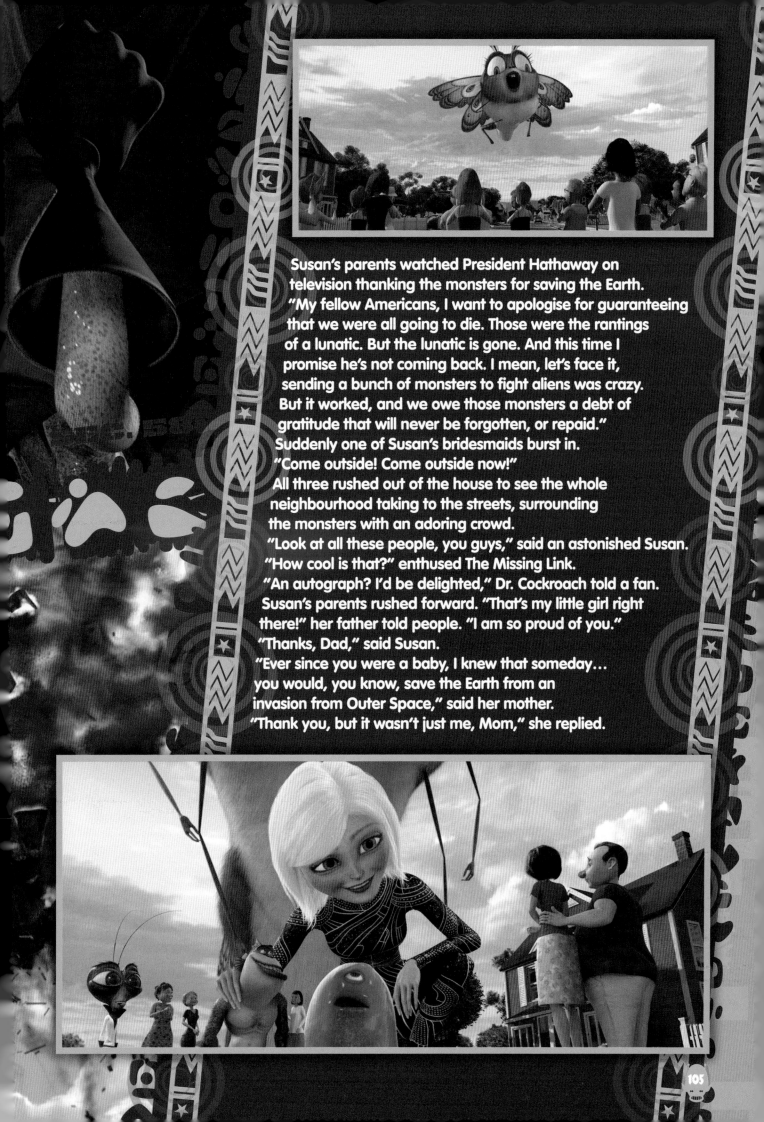

Susan's parents watched President Hathaway on television thanking the monsters for saving the Earth. "My fellow Americans, I want to apologise for guaranteeing that we were all going to die. Those were the rantings of a lunatic. But the lunatic is gone. And this time I promise he's not coming back. I mean, let's face it, sending a bunch of monsters to fight aliens was crazy. But it worked, and we owe those monsters a debt of gratitude that will never be forgotten, or repaid."
Suddenly one of Susan's bridesmaids burst in.
"Come outside! Come outside now!"
All three rushed out of the house to see the whole neighbourhood taking to the streets, surrounding the monsters with an adoring crowd.
"Look at all these people, you guys," said an astonished Susan.
"How cool is that?" enthused The Missing Link.
"An autograph? I'd be delighted," Dr. Cockroach told a fan.
Susan's parents rushed forward. "That's my little girl right there!" her father told people. "I am so proud of you."
"Thanks, Dad," said Susan.
"Ever since you were a baby, I knew that someday… you would, you know, save the Earth from an invasion from Outer Space," said her mother.
"Thank you, but it wasn't just me, Mom," she replied.

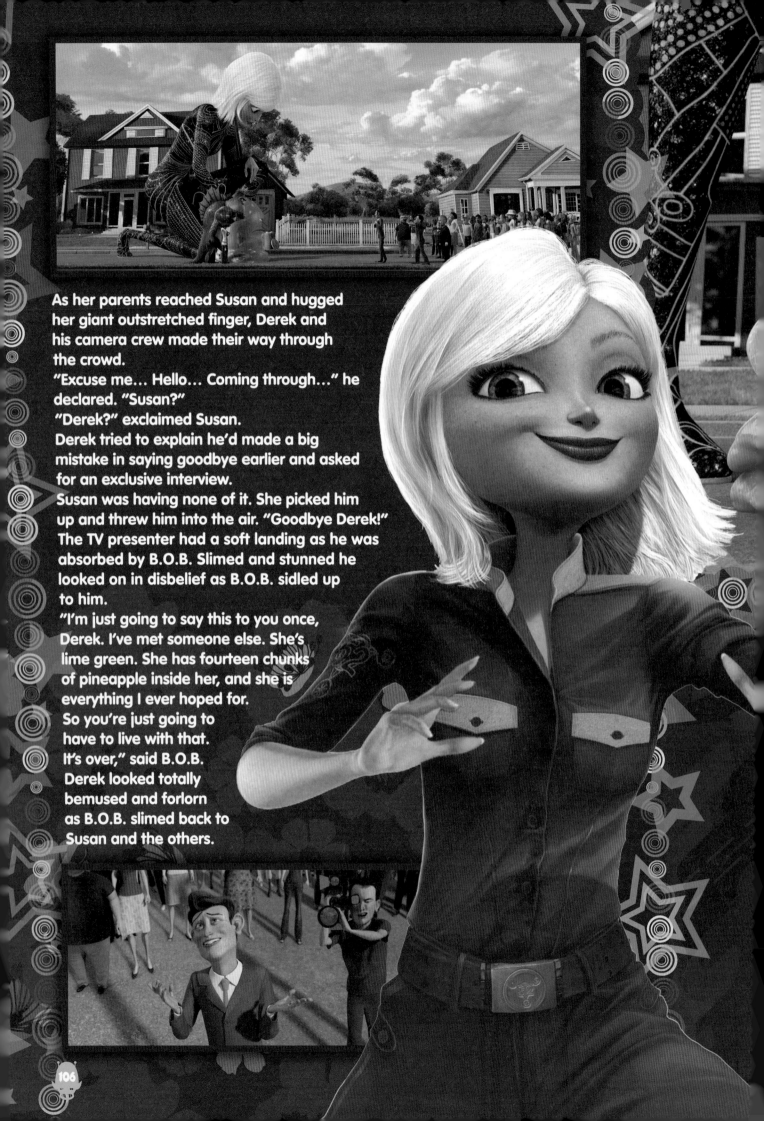

As her parents reached Susan and hugged her giant outstretched finger, Derek and his camera crew made their way through the crowd.

"Excuse me… Hello… Coming through…" he declared. "Susan?"

"Derek?" exclaimed Susan.

Derek tried to explain he'd made a big mistake in saying goodbye earlier and asked for an exclusive interview.

Susan was having none of it. She picked him up and threw him into the air. "Goodbye Derek!" The TV presenter had a soft landing as he was absorbed by B.O.B. Slimed and stunned he looked on in disbelief as B.O.B. sidled up to him.

"I'm just going to say this to you once, Derek. I've met someone else. She's lime green. She has fourteen chunks of pineapple inside her, and she is everything I ever hoped for. So you're just going to have to live with that. It's over," said B.O.B. Derek looked totally bemused and forlorn as B.O.B. slimed back to Susan and the others.

"Well, monsters, you saved the Earth and you're heroes," said a delighted General Monger, who handed them their freedom and packed them off to Paris. The monsters climbed on the back of the now butterfly Insectosaurus and he took off.

"Au revoir, sweetie!" called Susan's mother. "Have a safe flight!"

"Yeah! And hang on!" called her father as they flew into the setting sun.

"What's Paris?" asked B.O.B.

"I'll explain on the way," Dr. Cockroach told him.

"What's the way?" asked B.O.B.

"Really!" said an exasperated Dr. Cockroach.

ANSWERS

Page 24

S	A	N	F	T	E	N	T	D	O	H	E	E
U	U	P	R	O	L	L	E	A	C	A	N	N
S	A	R	O	A	C	O	B	A	N	T	O	D
A	T	E	U	S	H	C	O	C	O	H	A	R
N	O	G	R	A	H	X	A	L	L	A	W	A
B	O	N	A	I	S	H	T	I	L	W	O	L
A	B	O	T	L	B	O	B	N	O	A	L	K
S	I	M	I	S	S	I	T	E	A	Y	E	A
A	L	L	O	N	G	E	R	C	R	R	O	S
P	L	I	R	O	S	T	O	A	E	A	B	I
C	H	A	T	H	A	E	A	D	R	S	O	K
B	O	N	O	R	O	N	C	A	N	I	N	L
C	L	E	L	E	E	S	A	F	A	B	A	L
S	L	D	L	D	L	E	L	O	L	A	B	L

Page 25

Page 28

The catchphrases in the order that they appeared were: General Monger; Dr Cockroach; Gallaxhar; the Missing Link; B.O.B.; Susan.

Page 46

TSRPMLKHGD (write it in alphabetical order first and then reverse it); 9,000 seconds (60x60x2+1,800); five apples.

Page 50

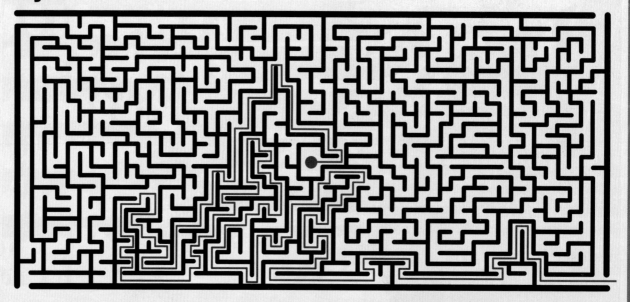

Page 68

FISH, WISH, WISE, WINE, WIND, WINK, LINK, LINE, MINE, MANE, MAN.

Page 69

B R I C K
M A G I C
G N O M E

B R A I N
S M O C K
S I N G S

Page 70

Save the Planet

Page 71

Pair 1 = A & D
Pair 2 = C & E
Odd one out = B

Page 89

Page 90

Page 91

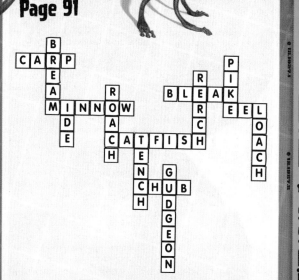

Page 92

1. Nemoy. 2. garter. 3. squidling. 4. fifty years. 5. a heart. 6. a jelly

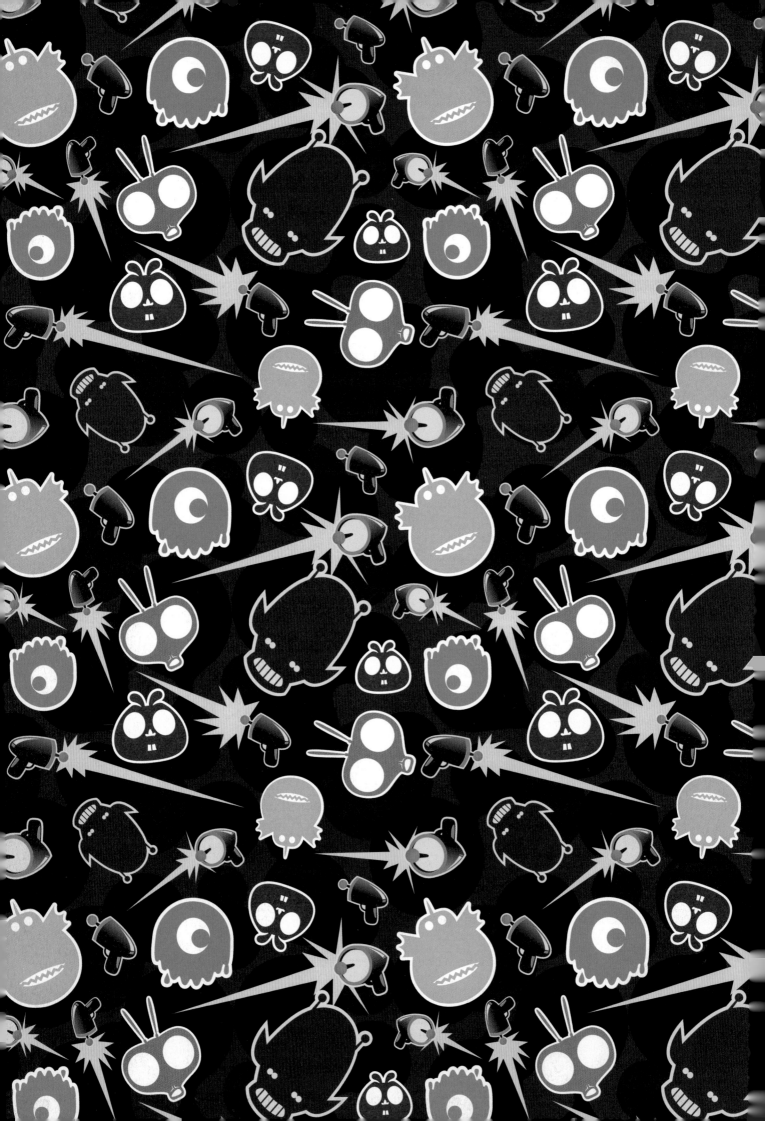